W9-BFV-656

NEARLY ALL THE MEN IN LAGOS ARE MAD

NEARLY ALL THE MEN IN LAGOS ARE MAD

* stories

DAMILARE KUKU

HarperVia

An Imprint of HarperCollinsPublishers

HarperCollins books may be purchased for educational, business, or sales promotional use. For information, please email the Special Markets Department at SPsales@harpercollins.com.

Originally published in Nigeria in 2021 by Masobe Books.

Published in Great Britain in 2022 by Swift Press.

FIRST HARPERVIA EDITION PUBLISHED IN 2024

Designed by Janet Evans-Scanlon

Library of Congress Cataloging-in-Publication Data

Names: Kuku, Damilare, author.
Title: Nearly all the men in Lagos are mad : stories / Damilare Kuku.
Description: New York : HarperVia, 2024. | Originally published in Nigeria in 2021 by Masobe Books. Published in Great Britain in 2022 by Swift Press.
Identifiers: LCCN 2023053420 (print) | LCCN 2023053421 (ebook) | ISBN 9780063316362 (hardcover) | ISBN 9780063316379 (trade paperback) | ISBN 9780063316386 (ebook)
Subjects: LCSH: Lagos (Nigeria—Fiction. | LCGFT: Short stories.
Classification: LCC PR9387.9.K85 N43 2024 (print) | LCC PR9387.9.K85(ebook) | DDC 823.92—dc23 / eng/ 20231115
LC record available at https://lccn.loc.gov/2023053420
LC ebook record available at https://lccn.loc.gov/2023053421

24 25 26 27 28 LBC 5 4 3 2 1

To Oluremi Abake
and
You who has dealt with a mad man
I salute you

CONTENTS

Cuck-Up   1

The Gigolo from Isale Eko   19

The Anointed Wife   33

International Relations   53

Ọdẹ-Pus Complex   73

A Lover's Vendetta   95

First Times   113

Catfish   137

Sidelined   161

Beard Gang   181

I Knew You   199

Independence Day   221

Acknowledgments   239

CUCK-UP

One night, you will calmly put a knife to your husband's penis and promise to cut it off. It will scare him so much that the next day, he will call his family members for a meeting in the house. He will not call your family members, but you will not care. You won't need them.

Your husband's family will crowd the new apartment—a bedroom and a parlor, called self-contain by Lagos agents—you got three months ago. It will feel like they surround you. They will exclaim, sigh, frown, click their tongues, gnash their teeth, and repeat a million times that you committed an abomination.

His potbellied uncle, Buraimo, who always leers at your bosom, will point at you and say, "Shebi I told him not marry you? I said marry someone from your tribe. Igbo women are dangerous." He will say this while ogling your bosom. "Well, I blame him for not handling you properly. Because if it was me who was handling you, ehn"—he will beat his chest in anguish at this point—"if it was me, you wouldn't have tried this nonsense."

His eldest sister, Azeezat, will pretend to appeal to your shared womanhood. "Isi, as a woman myself, I know men can be difficult. But what you have done is terrible. No woman has done this thing in our family. In fact, it is a disgrace to womanhood to want to cut your husband's member. Haba! If you cut Lukumon's member, how will you people have another child? You know we expect your next child to be a boy."

You will be so amused that she calls it member, it will make you smile.

They will misinterpret your smile.

"You are smiling at your evil, abi? You are not well! You hear me? You are mad!" Lati, his immediate elder sister with the tiny voice, will jump and bark at you before someone will tell her to calm down.

You will stay silent as you planned. Till your husband's older cousin, Mufu, the thief, will make you talk.

"Mufu, please bring out Lukumon's watch from your pocket, and put it back on the side-stool," you will say quietly, but with clear menace.

Everyone will turn to Mufu. Their embarrassed faces will confirm they know he's a thief. But because he's one of theirs, Uncle Buraimo will try to save his face.

"Mufu, eh, I know you were just . . . eh . . . admiring, eh . . . Lukumon's watch. But sha, put it back o, before she cuts your manhood."

They'll all titter, nervously, forcefully, while Mufu will pull the watch from his pocket and place it on the side-stool. He'll glare at you. You'll glare back and hope he gets the message that you'd no longer stand for him brazenly pilfering things anytime he visited, partly because Lukumon was scared to call him out.

You'll look at Lukumon and wonder how you came to love such a sorry excuse for a man.

You will remember when you were younger, when every man wanted you, but you fell for Lukumon's natural charm. You'll remember how he used to come knocking on your parents' door, leaving you sweets, and sweeter notes. You will wonder if your life would have been better if you had chosen the soldier with tribal marks from the barracks in Egbeda. The soldier loved you, but you'd chosen Lukumon, the beautiful man-boy who made you laugh and overfilled your heart when he said he loved you. You chose Lukumon because of his words—he wrote love letters, recited delicious poetry, whispered magic in your ears, and sang as you danced till you believed the lyrics of all the world's love songs were written just for you.

"God forbid you marry a teacher. You must do better than us," your father had said. But you were so possessed by love, you threatened your parents—to elope, to get pregnant, to kill yourself. It was your first and only rebellion, and they were so confused by it, they let you have your way.

"Isi, why did you threaten to kill my son?" Lukumon's mother's voice is soft, and her face impassive, as always. But you will remember she never liked or accepted you—she was just indifferent, and sometimes, it rankled more because you'd have preferred her to hate you. You will never say it, but you blame her and his five elder sisters for overpampering Lukumon. Yes, he was the last child and only boy, but their coddling contributed to making him lazy, entitled, and impotent in any adversity.

Before you answer, Kitan, your six-year-old daughter, will wake from her nap in the bedroom, come to the parlor, be scared of the crowd, spy you, and dash to your open arms. You'll hug her, carry her, sniff her neck, and enjoy her dusting-powder scent. She'll hug you tightly as if she knows you are under fire and she wants to shield you. She'll hold you till your heart warms. Till you'll say a silent prayer, for wisdom, for peace, for Kitan—that her life will be soft and she'll never leave you. You love her too much.

It was all for Kitan. You will remember your husband, when he was pressuring you and trying to convince you, had said, "Do this for Kitan."

You will look at him and your anger will rise red again.

But Kitan will rub your face with her cute fingers and calm your soul so you can tell your story.

You used to sell roasted corn at the junction of Unilag. When corn was out of season, you sold boli and sauce. Your business was fairly successful because your location was strategic, and there was a lot of foot traffic. Also, because you were punctilious with your business—in sourcing the freshest corn and plantains, in selecting the best charcoal for roasting, in preparing the sauce (with the famous boli sauce recipe from Port Harcourt), and in serving with neat newspapers and takeaway packs—you had many loyal customers. Lukumon said it also helped that you are friendly and you look like Naomi Campbell (people usually said the Naomi Campbell thing, but you'd never seen it, and frankly, it irritated you because you don't have Naomi Campbell money).

Selling roasted corn or boli was never the plan. You always thought you and Lukumon would make something of yourselves. But he lost his job a year after your marriage, and you had to leave your job as a secretary when you got pregnant. The aftermath of Kitan's birth was tough as you were both jobless, and your meager savings ran out. In those days, Lukumon sent you to ask Uncle Buraimo for money for food, and to get it, you endured the man bear-hugging you in greeting so he could crush your boobs against his chest. Eventually, you refused to go. It caused the first fight in your marriage, during which you flippantly said you'd rather sell roasted corn by the roadside than collect money from Uncle Buraimo. Then, weeks later, on a night after the landlord had made a scene because of overdue rent, a coaxing Lukumon reminded you of your words.

"It's just to bring a daily income while I'm job hunting," he said. "Mufu has talked to his oga at work about me. Hopefully, in another month or so, they'll give me a job. Just be patient, ife mi."

That was more than six years ago, but Lukumon still hadn't found a job. You'd sold corn or boli during that time and you didn't mind. It was honest work and provided for your family's basic needs. On average, you made about five thousand naira daily. Enough for food and rent for your family's one-bedroom face-me-I-face-you apartment. Enough to pay for your contraceptive pills because you both agreed not to have another child until you were financially stable. The only thing you paid a premium for was Kitan's education. You'd insisted that she attend one of the best private schools in Yaba.

Lukumon had argued that you were wasting money because Kitan could thrive in a public school and turn out well, just like he did. But you'd quietly said, "My child will never go to a public school in Nigeria as long as I'm alive." And he'd looked at your face, and never spoke of the matter again.

You met Ehi on a rainy Thursday in June, when he pulled up in his SUV to buy corn. He rolled the window down, "Madam, good afternoon. How much?"

You greeted him like you did everyone else. "Good afternoon, sir. Thank you for stopping. It's two hundred naira for one."

"Okay, give me five and six pears. Hope they're soft." "Yes, sir." You nodded, wrapped up his food, stood, and handed it to him through the window. He gave you five one-thousand-naira notes.

"Sir, your bill is only two thousand naira."

"I know. Keep the change. I like that you're very polite."

"Thank you, sir."

He returned two days later. This time, Kitan was with you as usual every day after you picked her up from school. He parked and got down. You studied him for the first time. He could have passed for average—his features, height, and build were average—but his clothes (well-tailored kaftan and designer slippers) and an air of brusque determination stood him out.

"Madam, your corn was so nice, I came all the way from Surulere to buy again."

"Good afternoon, sir. Thanks for coming again."

"Good afternoon, sir," Kitan said. As a rule your daughter greeted all your customers.

He beamed at her. "Good afternoon. What's your name?"

"Olaoluwakitan," she answered.

"Nice name. What does it mean?"

"God's wealth never ceases," you said.

He studied both of you for a moment. "Your daughter looks exactly like you."

"Thank you."

"You speak so well. What school did you attend?" There was a directness about him.

"Yabatech."

"That's nice. And how's business?"

"We thank God. We are pushing it." You were thankful he didn't ask how you'd ended up selling roasted corn by the roadside.

"Good. Oya, let me have the same order."

You added two extra cobs and five extra pears to his food. "Here, sir."

He collected it and gave you a wad of notes. It was fifteen thousand naira.

"Sir, please, I can't accept it."

He shrugged. "I won't take it back either." Then he smiled. "But I suggest you take it and buy something for Olaoluwakit . . ."

"Kitan. It's easier to call her Kitan." You smiled and thanked him as you took the money. It was enough for you to take the next three days off, but you didn't because you rested only on Sundays. But you did as he suggested and bought five dresses for Kitan: two new ones for church and outings, and three secondhand casuals for stay-at-home. She'd been wearing the same clothes for some years. And for the first time, impulsively, you bought her new clothes in her size. And when Lukumon, who you'd told about Ehi's generosity, asked why you didn't buy her new clothes two to three sizes bigger as you'd both always done, you said you forgot. As he frowned, you wondered why you couldn't explain to him that for once, you wanted to see your daughter in new clothes her size, rather than her growing into them when they were faded.

Ehi came to buy corn every week and always paid far more than for what he bought, especially when Kitan was with you. For a child who was usually wary of strangers, Kitan, surprisingly, had a lot of time for him. And it was because of the little things he did—always fist-bumping her, making funny faces with her, listening as she prattled about school and Lola, her best friend. You nearly cried the day he gave you two hundred dollars for Kitan. You thanked him and prayed for him, and you noticed he was uncomfortable.

He never stayed for more than twenty minutes, but you'd later realize that time was an escape for both of you. Over time, you developed a warm, understanding companionship of sorts. He didn't speak much about himself but you got to know some basics—he ran an international freight company, Ehioze was his full name, he was in the middle of a bitter divorce, and his two children lived with his soon-to-be ex-wife in London. Over time, you told him about yourself—first daughter of three of an ex-soldier and a military nurse, married to your first love, now mother of one.

You didn't tell him about Lukumon's unsuccessful job search till the day he asked what Lukumon did for a living. When you also told him, without prompting, that Kitan was always with you after school because Lukumon couldn't care for her while job-hunting, you realized it was untrue—Lukumon hadn't actively searched for a job in months, and spent his days idling at home. After you finished speaking, Ehi said, "If he doesn't mind, he can send me his CV through you, and I'll see what I can do. Let me know what he decides."

"Oh, thank you, sir."

"Please stop that. Call me Ehi."

At home, you told Lukumon about your conversation with Ehi, and asked for a copy of his CV. You were disappointed he didn't seem enthused.

"Okay," he said absent-mindedly.

"When will I get it?"

"Isi, you can see that I'm about to get on a queue to use the toilet. I need to get there before Ngozi messes up the place with her smelly shit. After that, I'll queue to take a bath. I hope I don't go in after that useless Alao, who uses two hours to bath."

"Okay, my husband. Give it to me when you finish."

"I have heard."

When two weeks passed and he hadn't given you the CV, you wrote one out for him, went to a business center to get it typed and printed, and gave it to Ehi. You didn't mind doing such things for Lukumon because, generally, he was a good man to you, just a bit lazy.

When you gave Ehi the CV, he studied it carefully. "I think I can fix your husband in somewhere in my company." Then, he looked intently at you. "What about you, Isioma?"

"What about me, how?"

"Do you want a job?"

"Not really, because it won't give me time to take care of Kitan. I want to take her to school and pick her up every day."

"So you're going to do this business forever?"

"God forbid."

You looked away. Then, because you'd grown too comfortable with him, you shared a plan you hadn't even told Lukumon.

"If I save enough money, I hope to open a grocery store to sell food items. There isn't one in my neighborhood, so I should have an advantage. I can get good produce from suppliers I know in Mile Two Market. Plus, I'll be closer to home and Kitan." You shrugged and sighed. "But it's just a dream for now."

"How much does your dream cost?"

11

You took a long pause before you answered. "I did a costing last month. Rent, furniture, and first stock came up to almost eight hundred thousand naira."

His face was impassive when he said, "Isioma, you're a beautiful woman. I want to help you, but I'm also human and selfish. So here is my offer—I will give your husband a job in my company. And I will give you two million naira. All I want in return is you spend this weekend alone with me in Osogbo. I'm going there for some business. Yes, this is a proposition. If you agree, you don't have to see me again after the weekend if you don't want to. If you reject my offer, I'll understand. But I suggest you think about it first."

How dare this man insult you? "Sir"—your tone was cold—"please don't buy anything from me again. I'm a married woman. My husband is man enough for me, and I'll never cheat on him. You've insulted both of us and—"

"It's an offer, not an insult," he deadpanned. Then his voice softened. "You have my number, Isioma. Think about it."

As he drove off, you felt a tear run down your cheek. You went home early.

You were still fuming when you told Lukumon about Ehi's proposition. You expected his rage to match yours, thunder to your lightning, but he stayed silent for a long moment. Finally, he asked, "Isn't that the man who gave Kitan two hundred dollars?"

"Yes."

"Foolish rich man."

"Yes."

Lukumon stood, grabbed a rumpled T-shirt from the clothes hanger, and pulled it over his head. It was the sign he was going out to play draughts with some of the men in the neighborhood. He paused by the door, "You're my woman. You will always be my woman no matter what. You understand?"

"Yes," you said, even though you were puzzled.

"Why do you want to kill my son?" Lukumon's mother will repeat her question and return you to reality.

You still won't answer. You will stroke Kitan's rough but soft hair, and make a note to loosen it, and weave fresh cornrows later. You will whisper in Kitan's ear, tell her to go play outside but not leave the compound. You will promise her sweets when she returns. Everyone will sense that you won't speak while Kitan is in the room. So they will stay silent, with bated breath, as she leaves, reluctantly.

Lukumon's shrill sister will be the first to speak. "Oya, answer Mummy's question. We are waiting."

You will make them wait.

On that Friday, your first night in Osogbo, Ehi made you wait.

Earlier in the day, he had taken you with him on his business, viewing tobacco farms he was considering buying on the outskirts of the city. He asked you to sit with him through meetings with landowners and farmers, introduced you as his associate, asked for your opinion, and asked you to take over the last meeting. When you returned to the city, he took you shopping, then to a late lunch.

In the hotel suite, there was an awkward silence as he sat on a couch and watched you perch uneasily at the edge of the bed. He asked if you wanted anything. You said no. He ordered a bottle of red wine and sipped alone. Then he asked for your account number. Ashamed, you replied that you didn't have a bank account (after you'd left your job as a secretary, you'd let your account go dormant, and couldn't even remember the number now). He asked if you had any ID. You said you had a voter's card and a national ID card. He called his account officer and told her he was going to send you with a check on Monday, and she should help you open an account.

Then he wrote and handed you a check—two million, eight hundred thousand naira. "For your dream, and then some," he said softly.

Though you were conflicted by it all and the extra money, you managed to retort, "For my soul, you mean?"

"I know this is hard for you, Isioma. In another world, I believe we'd be perfect for each other. But we're in this world, and the best we can get is this—this glimpse of what we could have been."

"I thought this was an offer. A transaction like the ones you do every day."

He sighed. "One of my many flaws is I negotiate for everything in this life, even for things that money can't buy. If I'd told you I think you're amazing, and I'm crazy about you, and I want you in my life, Kitan too—you'd have said no, right?"

Surprised, you nodded.

"That's why I negotiated for your crumbs."

You never understood why those words toppled your walls, eased your mind. So it felt natural when you both lay on the bed and talked, when he held your face and called you beautiful, when you kissed and tasted the wine on his soft lips and it all went to your head. A part of you was disappointed you only cuddled till you slept that night, but you understood he didn't want to rush you.

You woke the next morning alone in the suite. You went to the bathroom, washed your face, and brushed your teeth.

He came in, smiling and sweating in sportswear—he'd gone for a run. He took off his clothes and stepped into the walk-in shower. You smiled as you heard his off-key singing above the swish of the shower. He stopped singing when you slipped into the shower beside him, naked.

Silent apart from the kisses and moans, you washed and massaged each other first. You were both burning under the cold spray by the time you were through. Then he pinned you against the wall, and you lifted a leg to welcome him as he slid into you. For the first moment, he stayed still, while you felt and stared at each other. He started to move slowly, but with the poky space, and slippery floor, it got awkward quickly. You hurtled out and bounced on the bed still wet, water and body fluids. He lay on you while you wrapped your legs around him. He was amazingly different from Lukumon—savvier, kinkier, unselfish.

With your nipple in his mouth, his right hand gripping your left buttock, his left thumb caressing your clitoris as he settled into a thrusting rhythm, your racking orgasm was a pleasant surprise. As you pulled his hand from your clitoris because it was too intense, you realized that you both forgot to use a condom. Though you were on regular contraceptives, you preferred not to take any more chances. So you pushed him gently off you till his back was on the bed. You knelt between his legs, pushed them apart, cupped his balls, slurped his penis till he burst in your mouth and hand.

Later, as you lay on his chest, you were fascinated by how fast his heart was beating.

It was still beating fast on your last night together. "Stay with me," he whispered.

You stopped your light drumming on his chest.

"I mean, when we get back to Lagos, come and be with me. You and Kitan. I know my personal life is a mess, and your marriage is complicated, but I also know we'll be good together."

You don't speak for a long time. Then you exhale heavily. "You're negotiating again."

He chuckled. "I know. I don't know how to stop."

"I don't want you to stop."

Finally, you will answer your mother-in-law.

"Ask Lukumon," you will say.

Lukumon in the corner, with his head like a dried kola nut, will be startled to hear his name. He will reach for his watch, which Mufu had returned, and your eyes will meet. You will both remember that you bought the watch, an original Tissot, and the only luxury purchase from your windfall, for him because he'd always wanted one. You will wonder if, in the circumstances, his pride will let him continue wearing it. He will look away from you as he straps it around his wrist.

"What should I ask Lukumon?"

"Ask your son why he made me sleep with another man for money," you will say quietly.

Your words will suck out all the air from the room because nobody will breathe. Their eyebrows will raise, eyes widen, jaws go slack. Uncle Buraimo will put both hands on his head and throw both feet up. "Ah! Ah! Ah!"

"When I say he made me, I mean for three days, he quarreled with me, refused to eat my food, didn't touch me, and even begged me to do it to secure our daughter's future. He's here—ask him why."

Lukumon will stare at the ground, refusing to look at you.

"Lukumon, please tell your family why you made me sleep with another man for money, but treated me like a leper when I returned. Explain why you refused to take the job the man offered you, but you insisted that I took the money, rent this house, and buy you that stupid watch. Tell them why you have refused to touch me but you're sleeping with every girl in the neighborhood. Why did you say yesterday that you don't think Kitan is your child?"

You will take a deep breath and look your mother-in-law dead in the eye. "One last thing—if Lukumon doesn't move out of this house, I will cut off his penis and use it for money rituals."

Then you will smile.

THE GIGOLO FROM ISALE EKO

7:26 p.m.

I can see this is your first time at a bachelor party for Iggy?

How do I know? I organized the two previous ones and I didn't see you there. Yes, this is the third bachelor party I've thrown for Iggy. And knowing him, I suspect I'll throw at least three more for him before we grow old and die. Even worse, I fear my hell in the afterlife will be to throw bachelor parties for him every day for eternity. Be ready sha, because I'll invite you for all of them.

How do you know Iggy? You don't? A friend dragged you here? That's great. I'm happy you're here, and I think you're meant to be here, because in my experience, there're only a few random events in life.

How do I know Iggy? Ha! Iggy's like my brother. But no, that doesn't make me the best person to answer your question of why he keeps getting married? But if I was to guess, I'll say maybe he's looking for something he'll never find. Me, I don't know what it is sha. My own is just to organize the bachelor parties and turn up big-time at the weddings. Why? Because he's my Day One guy, and because it's what I do for a living. I organize music festivals and events; and I own a lounge that turns into a nightclub on weekends. The party never stops for me. So I'll throw a dozen bachelor parties for Iggy if he wants. But I swear, the biggest and best bachelor party I will throw will be for Seni.

Who's Seni?

You see that tall guy talking with Iggy? Ah, I'm glad you described him as handsome—you have good eyes. Yes, that's Seni. He's my guy and like my brother too. What's that? Seni has an aura of sadness around him? Hmm, I see you're perceptive. Why haven't I thrown a party for Seni? Because he's single. Yes, I mean single-single, never-been-married single. Hard to believe for such a correct guy, right? No, nothing is wrong with him. In fact, he's the best one of us, a gem of a man: any woman would be lucky to have him.

So why isn't Seni married? Hmm, it's a long story sha, and truth be told, a part of it is Iggy's fault. What happened?

Should I be telling you all this? You have a trustworthy face, and I'm a bit drunk, but still. Okay. Okay, stop begging.

To tell that story, our story, we'll need a full night and plenty of alcohol. Luckily, we have both. It's an open bar, so grab yourself a drink. Enjoy the party a little. I need to go check on the chefs and the kitchen. I'll be back.

9:34 p.m.

Hmm? I am sorry, I didn't hear you. Oh, you heard Iggy is marrying Pamela tomorrow for her money? Yes, I've heard that before, and frankly, I can understand why people will say that. Yes, she's wealthy: rumors say she's worth thirty million euros, inherited from her late husband, who was a mogul in the mining business. And there's the obvious, almost twenty-year age gap. Yes, I believe she's sixty. But Iggy insists he's not marrying her for money. He swears he loves her. Look, I've seen how he dotes on her. Do I think he's acting? If he is, he's fantastic at it, and he's probably done it for so long that the lines have blurred. Anyway, like I said, there're only a few random events in life.

Understand that Iggy has always been charming, even from childhood. We met in Isale Eko, Dosunmu Street to be exact. I know when people hear Isale Eko they think about three things depending on who they are. They think crime, Awori people, and slums. These things are all true. Isale Eko is an ancestral home of Lagos, and yes, it is now cluttered with poor housing and the streets are riddled with crime. But that's not what we are about. When you're truly from Isale Eko, you care about family, community. I'm not talking about the mummy-daddy-two-kids type of family. I mean ragtag, non-blood-related, bound-by-loyalty type of family.

Anyway, we met when we were both eight. His mother, Mama Perpetua, used to cook for my family during the festive seasons, and we all attended the same church, St. Joseph's. I remember seeing Iggy a couple of times, but we didn't speak till one day when his mother brought him to our house, and while she cooked, he wandered off without her knowledge and explored our house like he owned the place. I remember this because he walked boldly into my room and asked me who I was and what I was doing.

I was playing Ludo alone. I played by myself a lot because I was an only child, and I was shy back then. Anyway, without invitation, Iggy sat on my bed, picked the dice, shook them, and said, "My name is Iggy. Let's be friends."

And that was it. We became best friends and brothers. I say brothers because we became so inseparable, when I threatened to drop out of private school to join Iggy in public school, my mum offered to move him to my school. Eventually, my parents moved his family of three to our boys' quarters (BQ), but he was never there because we shared my room. Through the years, we shared everything else including clothes (though he coordinated outfits better, and carried himself with a certain style that always stood him out).

We also started chasing girls together, and again, he was

also a lot better at it than me. I remember when we were about eighteen, we used to sneak to eat at the legendary Iya Lati's buka in Tinubu Square. Men came for the delicious food and to ogle the girls, while women came to side-eye the girls who were taking their husbands, but couldn't resist the food. Many men lusted after Iya Lati's girls, but they all had crushes on Iggy. Usually, they were notoriously rude, but they smiled and fell over themselves to serve Iggy whenever he came. And his food got larger, even though we all paid the same amount. Then one of the girls started delivering food to Iggy at home. When I asked him about it, he just smiled. "Bro, na grace."

I didn't understand what he meant until about a week later when a big catfight—complete with flying pans, scratched faces, and torn clothes—broke out among Iya Lati's girls. It turned out that one of the girls, who considered herself exclusive with Iggy, had found out he was sleeping with three others.

Her name was Grace.

The first time Iggy got married was three years after National Youth Service Corps (NYSC).

That was young, right? But by then, he was already a big boy compared to most guys our age. Although he was a pure

Isale Eko boy, by the state-of-origin rules, he wasn't considered a Lagosian for NYSC posting. He used this to his advantage to work his posting to Lagos (I was posted to Enugu). During that one year of NYSC, he worked at a family-run logistics company, which surprisingly rented a furnished two-bedroom apartment in Lekki for him. He was still working there when I returned to Lagos after the NYSC year, and as bros, he asked that I move in with him. I did, and quickly discovered that he'd gotten all these perks at work because he was dating Folakemi, the oga's daughter, who ran the company.

They had a nasty breakup when Iggy switched jobs six months after NYSC and joined a fintech in Victoria Island. No, it wasn't simply because of the new job. He was headhunted by a senior madam in the fintech. And yes, you guessed right—he and his new madam had something, and Folakemi found out. Omo! Because she'd just renewed the rent for a year, Folakemi wanted to evict Iggy from the apartment. What saved him was the receipt and tenancy agreement were in his name. Also, the apartment was in a gated estate, so he told the security men to stop letting her in.

Those were crazy and wild days for Iggy, and us. I can't remember which lady bought him a BlackBerry (those were BlackBerry days), his work madam got him a Toyota RAV4 (codedly, of course), another woman took him on a vacation to Mauritius, some girl redecorated the apartment, and others kept sending food to us. Omo! Me and Seni were amazed by Iggy's moves. Seni? Oh, he and Iggy started working at the fintech at about the same time and bonded when they discovered they were fellow Isale Eko boys. Eventually, Seni moved out of his parents' house and into the apartment with us. He and I shared a room, Iggy stayed in the other.

Understand that this was about two years post-NYSC, and there we were, still boys at heart, not quite men, living the dream lives of young Lagos bachelors with the girls, apartment in Lekki, clubbing and barhopping on weekends. We developed some system: I identified the fun places to visit and the parties to attend; Iggy came with his car, some money, and his pool of women; and Seni, the calm and sensible one, kept an eye on us, protected us from thieving women and bar brawls when we got drunk, drove us home and carried us to our beds.

Anyway, Iggy's first marriage, right? So we're chilling at home one weekend, when Iggy comes and drops the bombshell that he's getting married. We ask: Dude, aren't you too young? Man said no. Okay. We ask: Which of your women? Man said: Odunola. We said: Who? We don't know this girl. Long story short, we got to meet her. Unlike the women Iggy liked to roll with at the time, she wasn't much of a looker. She was quiet, had no airs, preferred to blend into the background, but looked up to Iggy like he was God. We tried to figure out his angle, but he didn't say anything. He took her to meet my mum, who stood in for his mother (who'd passed on in his last year at uni). Even my mum wondered if he wasn't rushing things, but he said he knew what he was doing.

I threw Iggy's first bachelor party. And I'll never forget it. Not because it was a great party, but because it gave me direction. I mean there was a moment in the middle of it, I stood in a corner watching everyone dancing and having a good time, and boom, I had an epiphany—I could start a business for partying and events. And that's what I did. But that's another story.

Anyway, back to Iggy. So they had a quiet wedding next day. Her parents gifted them a duplex in Parkview where they moved into. Six months later, they moved to the US together, and he gifted me the RAV4. He was there for five years and though we kept in touch, it wasn't quite the same. Anyway, after five years, Iggy came back alone, divorced. Seni and I asked: Dude, what happened? Man said, nothing, they just drifted apart.

What's that? you asked. His angle for marrying Odunola? Well, he came back with an American passport sha, if that's what you're hinting at. Turns out she was an American citizen.

Anyway, like I said, there aren't many random events in life.

10:45 p.m.

Iggy's second marriage? Sure. I'll get to that.

First, we put the band back together like *The Blues Brothers*. Iggy, Seni, and I.

Some things stayed the same. Iggy and Seni started working together again, this time in their own fintech company, which they co-founded. Their company developed payment-processing platforms and solutions. Seni did the core tech and operations work; Iggy ran the marketing and business side. Their clients were mainly companies, and while they had some success and steady growth, I remember Iggy used to say they needed one big contract from the government to make a killing.

And some things were different. We didn't live together: I'd recently opened a lounge and grill in an old bungalow and moved into the BQ behind the bungalow because of the late hours I worked and so I could monitor my business. Freshly divorced Iggy did the same thing, by living at the converted BQ behind the duplex in Ikoyi where his and Seni's company operated from. Seni had retained the old apartment.

Every day after work, they came to my lounge/grill to hang out, and we had dinner and drinks together.

That was where we met Jamilah.

One evening, she came in wearing jeans, Converse sneakers, and a hijab—then she ordered takeaway pork chops like a teen boy buying his first condom. I must have smiled as I took her order and passed it to the kitchen, because she muttered: Don't judge me. And I said: I'm Catholic, it's Good Friday, and I've had both pork and lamb chops today. She smiled and said: Wow, you're going to hell. And I said: See you there. And we laughed. Turns out she worked at the ad agency down the street, had a weakness for the pork chops, and only came for the first time because the security man who usually bought them codedly for her wasn't around that day.

I convinced her to join our table while she waited for her order. She ended up having dinner with us, and she fitted in comfortably like we were old friends. It quickly became a thing for her to join us for dinner twice or thrice a week. There was something about Jamilah. No. Scratch that. There were many things about Jamilah. She was stunning, yes, but it was as insignificant to her as a yawn. There was a light to her, as if she could lift anyone's spirit with a listening ear and a warm smile. She was incredibly funny, got our jokes, and I can't explain how important this was. Forget sex and food— nothing steals a man's heart faster than a beautiful woman who genuinely laughs at all his jokes.

Seni was smitten. Iggy too, though he tried to play it cool. Me? Not really. I'd just started dating my wife then, but more important, I understood there was no point pining for Jamilah because the religious difference was always going to be a problem. Seni knew this too, but it didn't stop him from falling for her. Did he tell her? No. Did he try to date her? No. But they got so close, I remember some of my staff assumed they were dating.

Anyway, about six months after we met Jamilah, Iggy came to me one day and said he'd converted to Islam, and taken the name Iqbal. I couldn't place it, but I sensed this had something to do with Jamilah and it was going to go bad. So I said: Don't do this.

But man, acting all innocent, asked: Do what? So I said: Ignatius?

Man said: Yes.

I said: Your mother, God rest her soul, named you after St. Ignatius of Loyola: what the fuck is an Iqbal?

You can guess the rest of the story from here, right? Yes, the newly converted Brother Iqbal made his move, turned on his charm, and Jamilah agreed to marry him. It's one of those things I still can't understand because she knew who he was—I mean we were honest about his escapades when we all hung out, right? Or maybe, being in her early thirties at the time, she was under pressure from her family to get married and she had no other eligible Muslim men in her circle to vibe with. I don't know.

All I know is I was asked to do another bachelor party. Man said: Make it halal.

And I said: God punish halal!

Why? Because I never believed he was truly a Muslim.

Anyway, later I said to him: Look, I'm bringing strippers, a blackjack table, a roulette wheel, and enough alcohol to host a carnival in Isale Eko—if you like, come, if you like, don't come.

Of course, Brother Iqbal came. Seni didn't come though.

Seni? What do you think? Nothing was the same.

First, he'd tried to play it cool by congratulating them when their surprise engagement was announced. He even came to the wedding, and pink-eyed with pain, drank more than I'd ever seen him do, and for the first time in my life, I had to carry him and make sure he got home safe rather than the other way around. I spent that night with a broken man, and all he kept slurring was: I hope he treats her right.

He took a leave from the company after they returned from their honeymoon. He didn't return. He called me from Abuja to say he was transferring his shares in the company to me. A few weeks after, the shares became a lot more valuable. Turns out Jamilah's uncle, a devout Muslim, was a big shot at the federal revenue service, and through him, the company was given a contract to process incoming tax payments to the government for a percentage. This was the life-changing contract Iggy had hoped for the company and had finally gotten.

A cynic would say that was his angle for marrying Jamilah.

I also understood why Seni had given me his shares and walked away—any money made under that contract would have felt to him like taking a bribe to lose the love of his life. I took the money, but I've never touched it. It's in an investment account yielding interest. If I can't convince him to take it back one day, I'll use all of it to do something for Isale Eko people.

Our group? We broke up like P-Square. Seni stayed in Abuja. Me and Iggy weren't quite the same. I think the last time they saw each other before today was when they came for my wedding. But it was awkward. And the bastards didn't throw me a bachelor party.

Iggy and Jamilah? What do you think? The contract lasted for five years, till her uncle retired. Their marriage and Iggy's Islam held for a year after the end of the contract. Life has few coincidences.

I still call him Iqbal sometimes though. Just to fuck with him.

Incredible story, right? I hope it was worth listening to.

Seni and Iggy have spent all night talking? Oh, you noticed. Yeah. It seems to be going according to plan. They have a lot of catching up to do. Plan? Yes, the plan, my plan, is that they'll patch things up somehow, especially as Seni is moving back to Lagos. They don't have to be as close as before, but, if it happens, I'll welcome it. I miss my boys.

I think I started by saying there're only a few random events in life. Let me come clean with you. I hope you won't get mad. Your friend, who's also a good friend of mine, didn't just randomly drag you to this party. And I didn't just tell you all this for fun. The plan, our plan, is for you and Seni to meet.

Don't call it a blind date. Just a meeting. We think you'd both be perfect for each other, but no pressure. Just meet, have a chat. Come, let me introduce you. You can kill your friend later. And if this works out the way I suspect it will, you'll hug and thank her instead. I like that you're smiling and seeing the funny side.

What's that? If it works out, I shouldn't throw a bachelor party? You're killing my dreams, woman, but okay.

THE ANOINTED WIFE

Do you think it is easy to be a pastor's wife? How can you know what it means to be the partner of a man with a divine calling, made of flesh but instructed to lead with the spirit? Any ordinary wife has their work cut out for them in loving their husband, in serving them for richer or poorer, in sickness and in health, but a pastor's wife has to help her husband maintain his holy anointing, and to do so with an invisible hand.

"I didn't do it. Mummy, do you believe me?"

How long has it been since I became the mummy of our organization, the mother in our marriage? I can't remember. It feels like forever since I had the pleasure, the intimacy of hearing my own name fall from my husband's lips—my real name, not Mummy, sometimes followed by one of the children's names. I look at him now. His pleading eyes and downturned mouth. His hair is impeccably groomed, his salt-and-pepper beard neatly trimmed. We have been married for more than twenty years. Our love has gone beyond compassion, beyond butterflies in the stomach, and settled into a form of kinship. Tade and I are members of an elite, exclusive club; we couldn't be closer if we had shared some kind of blood covenant.

"Of course I believe you. I am working with Demilade from PR, my press release will be on our Facebook page within the hour."

He smiles broadly; it reaches his eyes and brightens his aura. He takes two steps toward me and, when he's close enough, reaches out and rubs my arms. Up and down. Three times. He stops when I pick up my notepad from the table to look over my handwritten letter. It is meant for the members of our church and the wicked, judgmental general public.

My dear hopefuls,
It is with a heavy heart that I write to you. As you go about your daily activities, please do not let the devil take hold of your mind with fake news. Two weeks ago, an article was released accusing pastor of sleeping with a young lady on the 19th of June 2020. The young lady claims that my husband, our daddy in the Lord, picked her up from Festac, took her to a hotel close by to have inappropriate relations with her. She says she is coming forward because she saw Daddy on television preaching and she didn't think that it was right for an adulterer to be the one to guide people on their spiritual journeys.

I am not saying this young lady is a liar but on the date that she claims they met, our daddy in the Lord and I were in the house with our three children rounding up a three-day weekly fast. We always round up this particular fast with a prayer and vigil, which is mostly heralded by our daddy. That evening, I led the prayer because Daddy had to rest his voice for the next day—we had a retreat for pastors all over Lagos. However, throughout the vigil, Daddy was with me, encouraging me and making sure that I never felt alone.

Hopefuls, I don't think you can know a person completely, but if my husband—our daddy in the Lord—was a twin, I think his wife of twenty years would know. Unless the young lady met my husband's long-lost brother that we have never heard of, then her claim of staying with Daddy throughout the night is false.

The society finds it easier to judge leaders—religious, political, academic leaders—but does anyone ever stop to think about the consequences of their judgment on these families? This media organization that published this article, Instablog, has had no sympathy for my family and me. Otherwise they would have reached out to us to confirm the young lady's claims.

My children are being mocked in school as the ones with the father that likes ashewos, the church lines have been ringing nonstop, and our daddy in the Lord seems to be struggling through all of these because he is human. This is why I decided to write this open letter to you all. To ask that you remember that we are human beings. We are flesh and blood. We are not equipped to survive social media slander.

I ask in the name of the most high that the blogs take down this article and that we stop attacking the church which is the body of Christ.

The young lady in question is a woman of the world who mostly moves at night. Is it not possible that under the influence of narcotics, she might have mixed up her sightings? Let us remember that only our Lord is blameless and without fault. This young lady may have just been seeing wrongly. She describes a car that is similar to that of our daddy in the Lord, which I ask—is our daddy the only man in Lagos with that car? Is the car manufacturer only making cars for my family?

Again, I am not condemning the young lady, because the kingdom of God allows for all types of people, in fact, we look forward to welcoming her in our fold and sharing the good news of the Bible with her.

Finally, please keep my family, the young lady, and I in your prayers as we all navigate through this difficult time.

I pray that the Lord continues to stay with us especially during these perilous times.

God bless you.

Pastor Mrs. Evelyn Oriade

I know what you're thinking. You think I'm wrong in supporting my husband, abi? Is it not a cliché at this point to accuse powerful men of scandalous things? Ordinary people enjoy the spectacle of watching those with a platform, a brand, a pulpit, fall. But I told you, I know Tade. I knew him when he was a gangly twenty-two-year-old with a concave chest and a beardless face.

We met in my father's small parlor church. I was eighteen. Although my father's foray into evangelism didn't pan out, my burgeoning friendship with the slightly older boy who had just moved into our area with his family deepened. Even then he was bookish and serious, while I was only pretending to be because of my strict parents. I knew that he would be safe to be around, and my parents wouldn't question us spending all our time together. While he was timid and reserved, I was wild and carefree. The first time I roughly planted my mouth on his and vigorously rubbed the area around his crotch he leaped away from me in surprise.

"Sister Evelyn!" He swiped the back of his hand across his mouth and scrambled to his feet. We were alone in his parents' two-bedroom house, studying at the dining table. There was no light and I was tired of waiting for him to pick up on every signal I had sent him before that moment when I took matters into my own hands.

"I'm not your sister. Besides, you're older than me."

He backed away as I stood up and walked toward him. He muttered something about this being wrong. So I said okay, I wouldn't do it again. But I did, two weeks later. This time we were in my house, downstairs by the door. We had a maid back then, and she was in the kitchen singing Igbo gospel songs. I used her singing voice to judge her location in the house, so when he turned around to say goodbye to me, I kissed him again. His back was pressed against the small section of the wall behind the door. I was gentler this time, softer. He didn't push me away and his lips closed warmly against mine.

After that, we kissed every time we were alone. Falling against each other with fevered passion. My rubbing against his groin became more practiced, and I was rewarded with a bulge that grew with each caress. One day, I couldn't take it anymore so I hiked up my skirt and got on top of him. I found the sweet spot between our bodies and I rocked my hips back and forth, the thin material of my underwear and the cotton of his trousers moistening. He moaned hotly against my neck, his hands fondling my breasts as he whispered my name over and over. Evelyn. Evelyn. Those moments felt like liquid ecstasy. But he never allowed us to go beyond that until we were married three years later.

So, you see? That prostitute is lying and she will soon be cast back into the pit of hell where she crawled out from.

The story did not die.

I should not have been surprised. Gossip these days is a

hot commodity, a quick path to wealth on the internet high-way. In the old days, rumors would circulate among friends and family in your area; in the worst-case scenario, it might reach another local government area or state. These days, bad news travels at the speed of light, leaping from one blog post in Lagos to London within seconds.

Several blogs reposted the original article, and within a week, the girl whose name I have refused to learn or remember had sat down with journalists detailing her alleged one-night encounter with my husband. I compared the metrics of my Facebook post and retweets of the church's official response to the bloggers and saw that we were losing. Badly. What? Are you surprised that I'm talking about losing? Do you think this is an ethical or moral war that this girl is waging against my husband? Of course not. This thing is all about PR. Even though she is a liar and a prostitute, the truth is, in this social media era we are in, the only thing that matters is who people believe, who they sympathize with. And right now, I am losing, but I won't be for long.

The task of being a pastor's wife is multilayered, like an onion. I have skills and weapons that you would not believe. Let's begin with my stylist. She makes sure that I am dressed head to toe in clothes and accessories that exude wealth with a hint of humility, outfits that skim my curves in a way that is attractive but not sleazy. My toenails are polished but not French manicured. I stick to warm colors and pastels, no

Ruby Woo for me. And what about social media? Our church's biggest audience is on Facebook, the masses, that's why my first press release went there. I use simple, common language to appeal to a sense of connection. We are all the same, after all.

On Twitter, I target the intelligentsia, I know the buzzwords and throw them around. Empowerment. Patriarchy. Community. These days I keep the comment section locked because I don't have time to argue, just inform. Then we have our PR outfit, a staff of five including a videographer. They film and edit our events, make sure to capture the special magic of our church services, with a splattering of intimate behind-the-scenes moments appearing here and there. It could be a shot of Tade rehearsing a sermon, or one of our children giving him a hug when he gets off the stage. It broadens our appeal, you see, humanizes us. These videos go on our YouTube channel. The team is hard at work now in the event of the so-called scandal to upload our latest service. We worked with an external crisis manager to make sure it hit the right note. Not too defensive, not sober enough to look like an admission of guilt. I manage them all. I haven't even mentioned our social media interns, the admin team, or the finance department.

Do you see what I mean?

I'm sure you're being cynical now. Why does spreading

the word of God need so much machinery behind it? Is this the Gospel or an enterprise, right? Look around you. The world has changed and will continue to do so. Are Tade and I supposed to don sandals and robes, beating drums up and down Lagos with dusty feet and cracked voices? Does that sound dignified to you? Would you even buy car insurance from someone who looks like that, how much more the word of God?

Anyway, I have decided to issue my second press release in this matter. Me and this girl have only just started.

Good evening my brothers and sisters,

I understand that a couple of groups had an issue with being addressed as hopefuls. I apologize, I used that term with the purest intention. However, since I am aware that many people are uncomfortable with it, I will refrain from such terms. I will now use "brothers and sisters," because I believe we are connected through Christ, and God is our father.

*It has come to our attention that the young lady in question has released an audiotape of her exchange with our daddy in the Lord, I am also aware of the fact that she has been offered a book deal—*My Life, and the Night with Pastor—*where she will detail her supposed sexual encounter with our daddy.*

I am reading all the comments on social media asking me to come out and have a sit-down with the young lady. I apologize in advance, as I will not be able to do that. The Bible says that we must flee from all appearances of sin and we should not be equally yoked with unbelievers. I strongly believe sitting with a woman of the night is an insult to our Lord and Savior.

I stand by my husband and I am sad to see people doubt the word of a man of God and his wife. What will it profit us to lie? If my husband truly slept with the young lady, he will come out, repent, and retire from the church. This is the rule that has been laid down. There is no severe punishment for adultery because Jesus Christ has paid for our sins, so why will Daddy lie if there is no punishment? Yes, it may affect our public image, but that can be fixed through Jesus Christ and rehabilitation.

My husband did not sleep with the lady in question.

The tape recording may have been doctored; we live in a world where technology can and will do most things. What is voice copying in a world filled with Photoshop, Auto-Tune, and filters? It is possible this woman found a way to re-create our daddy's voice.

It is also shameful that a publishing firm agreed to publish a book like this. They didn't think about the children that would have access to the pornography in the book or the families that would be affected. Again, we must move and act with empathy. We are living in a world filled with selfishness and sexual perverseness. We must protect ourselves and, most important—our children.

Beloved, my husband does not know this woman and he has never stepped out of our marriage.

I will like to thank you all for your support and I am aware that there is a debate online about the credibility of the lady due to her profession. Please be gentle with her. She may be spreading lies but she is still human.

God bless you. God bless the blogs perpetrating this evil, and God bless the young lady who has allowed the devil to use her to destroy a family.

Good night.

Pastor Mrs.

Did I forget to mention the thing that drew me to Tade in the first place, besides the convenience of his harmless appearance? His voice. You need to hear it to understand. The first time he spoke to me outside my father's house after service it did something funny to my insides. I don't want to blaspheme but his voice is golden, God-tainted. And he seemed completely unaware of it.

When we were both in the university—he was studying accounting at Ife and I joined him there to study mass communications—the student unions regularly organized debates between departments, and that was where "shy" Tade shone. His voice was one part of the deal, but he had unbridled charisma. The seriousness that made him stiff off-stage became something commanding and authoritative on the stage. When he talked, people listened.

A year after we got married, I had our first child, Mayokun. Tade was managing a small clerical job in Yaba and things were tough. Without our parents, we couldn't have made it through those first three years with two children. I often left them with my mother and worked as an assistant in a small radio station, scraping by. One day I said to him,

"Tade, I think the church is your calling."

I analyzed my reasoning, told him why he would excel at it, and that he was the kind of man that should lead people. He looked at me with gratitude in his eyes and said he had been thinking the same thing. But he didn't know if I wanted that life because of how I'd grown up.

"We won't do things the way my father did," I had said.

While we both worked and raised our children, we built our church. We had ten faithfuls at first, and then a hundred. We designed our logo together. Filled up our vision board with milestones and goalposts. Our church's motto, "Work for God and for yourself," came from him and surmised our experience at the time. Two years later, after the birth of our last child and only daughter, he started earning better at an investment firm, and I took on a position as secretary at the local government office in Alimosho. It was a strategic choice. My job helped me find followers but it was also close to our children's school and home.

It has taken thirteen years to build this church from the ground up, and while I help run it, Tade still has a job. I handle everything so he can step on that stage and shine like he was born to do. Our main selling point, the reason why we have grown over the years, is my husband.

We have everything we ever dreamed of, and more. We live in a six-bedroom mansion in the heart of Akowonjo, Egbeda, with a cook, driver, and a gardener. Our three children go to exclusive schools—Mayokun recently got accepted to an Ivy League school in America. Tade and I did this together, and there's no way I will sit back and watch a nonentity destroy it all with her loose words.

As the weeks went by the scandal grew wings and added jet-pack fuel. I had to sit through interviews she gave to all and sundry, watch her lower her overfilled eyelashes in false modesty, her overflowing cleavage clearly showing who she really is—an opportunist and a gold digger. I watched and read every single thing this girl said because knowing your enemy is the first step to destroying them.

"Mummy, you don't have to do this," Tade says as I walk into our bedroom at 11 p.m. I had just put the lid down on my

MacBook in my home office after watching yet another video. I look at him and sigh.

"It's my job, Daddy Mayor." I preferred using the nickname of our firstborn when referring to him in private. That way, he felt like my husband, the father of my children, like someone that still belonged to me and not the world.

"Is there anything I can do to help you? Just tell me and I will do it. Should I appear on camera denying the claims?"

I sit down beside him and take off my shoes, rubbing the soles of my feet. Even when I work from home, I dress the part.

"No, there's no need. People will twist everything you say and it will make things worse. Let me handle it. It's my job."

He puts an arm around my shoulder and pulls me close. My mind wanders to the clip I had just watched. It is hard to believe the Tade that she described is the one next to me now. She said he was "wild, unbridled, and insatiable," and that is how I know she is lying. Even in the early days, Tade was quiet and reserved in bed. Now, after twenty years, we have sex only once a week or whenever the Holy Spirit leads him. It is time, my dear, let us go and celebrate the Lord in bed, he would often say before sex.

I feel sorry for the girl. Didn't she know that a lady never speaks about such matters in public? Well, she was no lady but still, I wanted to snatch her from the screen, put her across my knees, and spank decency, decorum, and coyness into her. Instead, I had watched with no expression with the

46

PR team because I knew if I gave away a hint of distress, Tade and the church would suffer.

Tade removes his arm from my shoulder and kisses my cheek. He returns to his side of the bed and within minutes is fast asleep.

Fellow Nigerians,

God bless us all as we take time to read this letter. I have received criticism about my tone of familiarity in addressing you all so I hope the title "fellow Nigerians" sits well with you. I have also received letters asking that I sit with the young lady, and to read the excerpts from her forthcoming book. On that issue, I will be granting an interview soon.

It is safe to say that this young lady is exploiting every opportunity presented to her to ruin the institution and body of Christ. My husband does not know this woman. He has never met her and he has confirmed this to the church and myself publicly and privately. This makes me wonder whether the church is not under heavy attack from the kingdom of darkness. I am beginning to fear for Christianity as a whole in Nigeria. Journalists, social media influencers, and any individual with a subscription can and do use their voices to stamp out the voice of our Lord Jesus Christ. I am grateful that there are so many people and believers that are standing with us during this crucial time.

She is now asserting that the church is preventing her book from being sold. I ask how? This story came out two months ago and she already has a book about to be published? Is it possible that the public can see through the loopholes in her story themselves and have decided to keep silent?

The church will not prevent anyone or dissuade them from buying the book.

Please tune in on Saturday as I sit with my dear brother— brother Chidi—to address the matter.

My husband does not know this lady.

Only Jesus does and only Jesus will deliver her.

God's blessings upon us all.

Pastor Mrs.

I have to hand it to this girl. Maybe I felt sorry for her for a moment, and I have definitely underestimated her, but whoever is helping her is some sort of marketing genius. Before they have even released her cursed tome of shamelessness, the excerpts have been flying up and down social media and communication platforms. I know that all the church ladies, family, and friends that have been supportive this whole time have read them. How? Their "Na wa o" now has a ring of sarcasm and mockery, the "God will handle this matter" sounds trite and condescending. And by accusing the church of trying to silence her, she has caused people who might not have supported her to come over to her side.

There is a PDF file open now on my phone screen. The impressions from the tweet that I pulled it from is in the millions. It describes some of the sexual encounter she had with my husband.

He tied my arms to the bedposts and spread my legs. He dipped his fingers into a bottle of oil which he called "the anointing oil that will break the yoke" and rubbed it on my clitoris and then he crawled in between my legs and whispered against my pussy.
"I have come to worship at your temple."
He started to lick me and then he grabbed my thighs, wrapping them around his neck.
"I want to be delivered! Deliver me, sister!"
I must confess I had never seen this kind of display in a man so I was unsure how to react. I just lay there and stared up at the ceiling. He finally finished his self-exorcism and thrust his erect penis into me. As he moved in and out of me, he kept saying, "We are celebrating the Lord in bed."

I place my phone facedown on my desk when I read that last line. I look up at the ceiling, but it does not stem the tears in my eyes. The girl might be a prostitute, but she is not a liar.

Is it accurate to say that I have caught Tade cheating on two occasions, if he doesn't know?

The first time was a year and a half into our marriage. I was supposed to be away for two weeks in Mushin to see a bereaved aunt. A week into the visit, the locust beans smell in her house and her constant whining drove me back home early. Mayokun was sleeping on my back and I had come in through the kitchen door because I had some foodstuff to offload. Tade's moans floated from the bedroom. For a moment I doubted that those sounds could be coming from my house, not to talk of my husband. I tiptoed to the bedroom and put my ear against the door. The creaking bedsprings and squelching of sexual organs painted a picture confirming the impossible. My fingers hovered by the door handle. Hot rage and humiliation surged through me. I wanted to jump into that room and claw his eyes out. Then I remembered that Mayokun was asleep on my back. Whatever I saw if I walked into that room, my innocent child would also see. I backed away silently and fled.

At the bus stop nearby I sat on a bench as my heart raced and my eyes darted about in confusion. How long had he been doing this? What did I do wrong? Maybe it was because we hadn't been having sex regularly since Mayokun was born. But he had been so understanding as I waited to heal from the stitches from his birth. I placed a hand on my chest to stem the dull ache that suffused my heart and let the tears fall. After thirty minutes, I went back home.

A young woman snuck out the front door just as I approached our home. She had all the telltale signs of what she was—a prostitute. She was nothing like me. When I walked into the house, it was as if I had imagined the whole thing. Tade was so happy to see us even though we were home unexpectedly. I wanted to say something, but the words never came. So I pretended not to know. And believed it was a fluke.

The second time was five years ago, late at night in his office. I had gone to surprise him because his firm had just completed a project he had supervised. He told me over the phone that he had some things to wrap up and he would be home late. The office complex was deserted when the security guard let me in. Later, I would wonder if the guard knew, and if he laughed at me for being naïve.

Upstairs, the door to my husband's office was slightly ajar and, for the first time, I got a clear view of Tade having sex with someone else. He had her on his office table, her cheap dress pulled all the way up and bunched around her chest to expose skin the color of an overripe guava. His hands held her legs apart at the knees. Her French manicured nails dug into his shoulders, the knuckles of her fingers three shades darker than her skin tone. Pooled around his feet were his expensive tailored trousers. His buttocks contracted as he slammed into her like a demon from hell.

Again, I walked away and didn't breathe a word of what I had seen to a single soul. After that day, I kept spies around him, who informed me of his whereabouts. When I got no reports of such a scene after all this time, I thought he had finally come to his senses. I was wrong.

I'm not a saint, neither am I a robot. It hurts to act like I don't know that the man I have given everything that a woman can give repays that devotion by chasing such a cheap high. I have wondered whether this peculiar habit is an addiction. I have fasted and prayed and I thought that something had finally shifted, and that one day, Tade would see me once again as just Evelyn, not Mummy, not some untouchable anointed wife.

I wait until the day before her book launch to serve her my last card. It is the CCTV footage of our family praying together on the date and the time that she claimed they had met. Of course, it was doctored, a deep fake. The team doesn't even know about the IT guy I found from Russia whose service I paid thousands of dollars for.

Tade had gone out that night, but I didn't doubt him until I read the excerpt. Yes, he has lied to me, cheated, but I've told you, what we have is beyond understanding and will not be allowed to fall.

INTERNATIONAL RELATIONS

I'm tired of Lagos men.

Nearly all of them are mad. Awon weyrey! The standard Lagos Man package comes with lying, cheating, and occasional scamming; alongside stylish kaftans, splashes of Sauvage or Ouds, and fake accents. See, they've shown me so much pepper in this my short life, I've finally seen the light—it's bright, and so white. By white, I mean oyibo. Yes, I'm going international and not looking back. I swear, the next man I date in this Lagos will be an oyibo: so help me God.

In this life, you need to know yourself. I have come to know myself. I have a sharp mouth, but I'm really a chilled-out woman. I don't like wahala, and Lagos men come with wahala in abundance even in little things. For example, I prefer to sleep by 10 p.m., but it's like that's morning for Lagos men. Talmbout, *the night is still young, let's go get something to eat*. Uncle, you and who will eat this late night? If I get fat, you will be the first to ogle and chase fitter girls. Plus, my parents both had high blood pressure, and since I'm genetically likely to get it in the future, I need to cut out one of my risk contributors—no, not food, Lagos men.

I used to be one of those girls who judged Nigerian women dating white men in Lagos. "Are there no guys in Lagos? Why are these fine girls sticking to these men?" I'd often complain to my friend Susan. She understood. Most of them were unattractive, middle-aged and older, and lacked even a drop of swag when compared to Nigerian men. Some smelled of garlic sef.

Then I began to really notice the women. I saw them as they paraded Lagos with their red-faced, potbellied oyibos. Many had that look, like they knew a secret which we didn't. Some looked smug around their men as if they were saying, This one is mine. He's going nowhere. No juju or punani can't take him away. Me sef, I wanted that assurance. In parties and other events, they didn't participate in that subtle jostling for the attention of Lagos men like we did. They always seemed content and self-assured, secure in their peace of mind and soft lives. Me too, I realized that peace of mind and soft life will fit me die. That's when I said to myself, ah, Shike, you have misled yourself and walked in error all these years.

So I decided to get myself an oyibo man.

I have a list of preferences.

First, he mustn't have a poverty mentality like one of my exes, Nonso, who insisted I always cook even when I was exhausted (because it was cheaper). It was a problem because he was one of those I-want-fresh-soup-every-day men. He called himself a foodie, but he was really a glutton. He fired my chef and my gardener as part of a series of silly wife-material tests. Me too, a mumu at that time, I was mute and didn't tell him I was skeptical about marriage (as the only child of deceased parents, there was no one to pressure me into marrying, and I preferred to keep it that way). My relationship with Nonso had me cooking, doing his laundry by hand, and cleaning on weekends; all tasks I'd rather outsource. Then he made me take Uber or public transportation when we went out, because he didn't have a car and, weirdly, he refused to enter mine. He didn't even want me to Uber to his house because he didn't want people assuming that men were dropping me off at his. So I'd either take a painted taxi or stop the Uber several houses away from his and walk down. I regained my senses and broke up with him the day he suggested we fly an okada over Third Mainland Bridge due to traffic (maybe it was also because we were on our way to see his mother, and I'd realized I couldn't take that huge step with such a miserly man).

Which brings me to my second preference. He should have his own money. I'm no longer lending money to any man or funding a man's lifestyle in this Lagos. As my late grandmother, my Iya Agba, would say, I'm better off using that money to play kalo-kalo.

I would also prefer my oyibo to be ugly or at least plain-looking. I want him to be grateful for dating me. I'm not really sure why I want this—maybe it's my vanity or the trauma of the infidelities of fine Lagos men who think they're doing women favors by sleeping with them. All the handsome Lagos men I dated ended in tears. The latest one was Andrew, who introduced himself as Dre, and looked like he was created by all the filter and model gods of Instagram. I'd stare at his chiseled body and wonder, and at his piercing eyes and want to confess sins I hadn't committed. He was twenty-five, four years younger, but he was so beautiful he made me break my rule of not dating someone I was older than. However, I quickly realized we were at different places mentally. All he wanted to do was smoke weed, take pictures for his social media, and go wild at clubs.

Also, I couldn't keep up with his youthful energy. I prefer gentle lovemaking. Andrew fucked like we were bitter enemies fighting to the death (and maybe that was partly why I refused to call him Dre). The first time, he even refused to use the bed. We did it against the wall, against the bedroom door, and on the cold tiles of my bedroom floor (I got a rug two days later). One time, he lifted my legs and crossed them mid-air. I stopped him immediately. "Andrew, only witches cross their legs like this. Free me." He'd send pictures of different sexual positions he wanted us to try. I kept thinking, *No, we mustn't try everything in the catalogue. I don't want to strain my joints to climax. And no, I can't twerk on your dick. I've got weak knees.* Sex should be jeje, easy. Miss me with all that freaky and overadventurous stuff. Even a core traditionalist like Nonso, who acted like the custodian of culture for his umunna, wanted to role-play as a little girl in bed. Ah! I told him it was an abomination in my place and kept it moving. So my fourth preference is that my oyibo should be conventional in bed.

I started my search in Ilupeju.

According to Susan, the best places to look for white men in Lagos were Ilupeju, Ikeja GRA, Lekki, and Ikoyi. My plan was to visit and spend some time in these neighborhoods on weekends. So, one Friday night, I decided to do some of my grocery shopping at supermarkets in Ilupeju. I whiled away a lot of time strolling through the aisles.

Amazingly, that night, I only ran into hot white men. *So,*

fine oyibo plenty for Lagos? Why were these women only following the wor-wor ones? I considered giving my number to one bearded and green-eyed hunk who was checking me out in a supermarket aisle, but I checked myself when I remembered my preference for a plain or ugly man.

I scheduled Ikeja GRA for the next day. Susan had said we should go to a restaurant frequented by oyibos. I called her that morning. She seemed surprised. "Shike, you are serious about this search?"

"Of course. What time are we doing dinner at this restaurant?"

"Seven p.m."

"Okay. Are you coming with your husband? Let me know so that I'll prepare myself for his lectures about marriage."

She chuckled. "Don't worry. Bayo has traveled. It's just me, you, and the girls." The girls were my other friends, Tolani and Bukky.

It turned out to be a Lebanese restaurant. However, I wasn't impressed by the crowd of mostly Lebanese men. The girls chuckled when I whispered, "Lebanese no be oyibo!" They all disagreed with me and we play-argued the point in Yoruba. We forgot about it when the food came, and we focused on gorging on the delicious feast.

Then, while waiting for the bill, a middle-aged Lebanese man with slicked-back hair rose from a nearby table, walked to us, smiled, and said, "Bawo ni. Oruko mi ni Sameed."

We howled.

In perfect Yoruba, Sameed declared I was right that Lebanese people weren't oyibos (but admitted with a laugh that many didn't mind being seen as oyibos in Nigeria). He explained that in the six years he'd been in Nigeria, he'd grown fluent in Yoruba and Pidgin, and was learning Igbo. He was bemused by my search for an oyibo, and said he'd like to take me out sometime. I reminded him he wasn't oyibo. He laughed, offered me his card, and paid our bill. We never spoke a word of English.

In the car, amid the cackling, Susan and the girls wondered why I hadn't given him a chance. I was amazed. "Wo! Did you hear his Yoruba? He speaks better than me sef. How will I keep a secret from him? See ehn, that man will be worse than any Lagos man."

And that was how I added a new preference to my list.

My oyibo should be Western. No Lebanese, or Indian, or Chinese, or anyone more Nigerian than me.

Week 5
I'm tired of searching for available oyibo men in Lagos.

It's been over a month, I've been to every major part of Lagos, but I haven't had any luck with finding my spec. Sometimes, I have this silly thought that this is the Universe giving me my comeuppance for all the oyibo boys I refused to give the time of day during my uni years in the UK. Ah! Jòó. E ma binu.

I'd focused on Lekki in the second week. Tolani had suggested that I stay at her place in Lekki for some days and join her on her daily jog on the Lekki-Ikoyi Link Bridge. Initially, I balked at the idea because I'm too chill for the wahala of exercise.

"Do I really have to run? Can't I just sprinkle water on my face and cleavage and act like I just ran?" I asked. However, the girls mocked me for being unserious till I bought matching sportswear and joined Tolani one cold harmattan morning. My luck was horrible. I gassed out after five minutes, developed a cramp at the back of my thighs, and didn't see a single oyibo. Worse still, as I trudged the bridge in self-pitying misery, I heard someone call my name from a passing car. It rolled to a stop ahead, parked, and Jimi, one of my exes, swaggered out with a smug smile. I wasn't in the mood for his games, so I told him straight up, "Well done, Olujimi. I've noticed you're driving a Bentley. That's why you stopped, abi? Oya, come and be going."

The foolish man sneered with his fake posh British accent, "I see you're still pretending to be razz."

So I laughed. "I see you're still borrowing people's cars and pretending to be rich. Meanwhile, shebi you've forgotten you still owe me money? Onigbese, when am I getting my money?"

Embarrassed, he turned, pretended not to hear me as he brisk-walked to the car and zoomed off in a huff. That was the end of my exercise and search for oyibos in Lekki. Two weekends later, I went to a restaurant in Ikoyi which Susan and Bukky swore by. Like they'd advised, I went alone and timed my visit to coincide with the oyibo crowd who came for long Sunday lunch. I found a table, settled in, but didn't order a starter immediately. Instead, I whiled away time sipping a Moscow mule and rereading Ayobami Adebayo's *Stay with Me*. I caught the glances of most of the men, and after some time, it seemed I'd lucked out because a man shuffled to my table. He looked exactly my spec—stocky, limp brown hair, plain enough, flaccid belly which jiggled under his T-shirt, and thin K-legs which looked awkward in his shorts and palm slippers. I could see in his eyes that he was nervous, so I smiled.

He smiled back. "Hello. May I join you?"

I smiled my answer, and remembered my Iya Agba used to say, sometimes men are like babies who you have to pull by the ear and show the way.

He started well. "You're beautiful."

"Yes."

But he didn't continue well after the introductions (his name was Uwe, he was German and an engineer). Somehow, he started talking about formation evaluation and reservoir simulation while I smiled and pretended not to be bored. And honestly, I didn't mind him being boring and having no game. I'd begun to think he was perfect but the

Universe had other ideas because, thirty minutes later, I noticed a white woman with stunning silver-blond hair come in and scan the room till her eyes locked on Uwe . . . and me. As she stronged her face, I knew immediately she was his wife or girlfriend. She strode toward us, and I thought, *Mogbe! Which kain wahala be this?*

Luckily, he spotted her, jumped awkwardly to his feet, and caught up with her before she reached the table. As he herded her toward the patio and outdoor section of the restaurant to lessen the embarrassment, I heard her berating him in their language and I was pleased. I refuse to fight over a man in public or private. The embarrassment still touched me sha because other diners noticed what happened, and it killed my chances. I quickly grabbed my things, called for the bill, paid (even though I noticed the waiter had included Uwe's half-drunk beer), and left.

Anyway, that's the story of how I bought a beer for a man who was trying to deceive me.

Week 7

One day, the Universe threw me a curveball in the shape of the Russian.

I'd met him when I was an adviser in consumer and industrial markets for one of the Big Four audit firms, and he headed a multinational waste and plastic-recycling company. I'd written a market intelligence report for his company through my firm, and six months later, it helped his company secure a lucrative contract with the government. To celebrate, he'd insisted on taking everyone involved to dinner, but by then, I'd left the firm for a better-paying rival. He'd gotten my number from my former colleagues and called me to join them at a restaurant in Victoria Island, but I was home in Gbagada and didn't fancy driving back to the Island. That was how I got his number, and because I only knew his surname, Mr. Zherdev, I saved it as "The Russian." After I'd settled in at my new firm, I wanted the Russian's company to hire us to provide audit and financial services. So I called him and scheduled a meeting for the pitch. I went alone because I didn't want to share any bonus my firm would give for securing a new high-net-worth client.

On the day, I got to his office at Ikoyi early. I presented myself to his secretary, a bony and thin-lipped woman with a bitter smile. "Good afternoon, ma'am. Shike Macaulay to see Mr. Zherdev. I have an appointment."

"Ah, I remember you." She sized me up for a moment, then whispered, "Still Ms. Macaulay?"

"Is that a problem?"

She half-sneered. "Don't worry. God will do it for you."

As I considered telling her that God should first focus on fixing her stupidity, the Russian opened the door of his office, poked his head out, and beamed. "Shike! Shike! Come! Come!"

He was grizzled, had stubble and gray eyes which crinkled when he smiled, and he smiled a lot. His handshake was firm and he held my hand for a moment and accused me in his halting English. "You help me get big contract, but you disappear before I thank you. Why?"

Without missing a beat, I said, "I know how you can thank me. Give my firm some work."

He chuckled.

"It's not just about thanking me. It's in your company's best interests to use my new firm. Allow me to show you why."

"Sit?" He pointed to a chair.

We sat on opposite sides of his desk, and he listened as I delivered my carefully rehearsed spiel. When I was done, he flicked through my firm's glossy brochure. Then he drummed his fingers on his desk and furrowed his brow. "Let me think this, okay?"

"Yes, sir." I said this in Russian.

He looked bemused. "Why you speak Russian?"

I said the truth. "I learned some Russian phrases from YouTube hoping to impress you and seal this deal."

His hearty laughter threw his head back and made his shoulders dance. He wiped tears from his eyes, leaned forward, and whispered. "I'm Ukrainian."

There was little I could do but laugh at myself. I was laughing when he asked, "You have boyfriend?"

"What?"

"Boyfriend. You have?"

"No."

"Good. Have dinner. With me. Please."

"Erm. You're my client. Okay, not yet my client, but . . . You understand what I mean? It's unprofess—" I exhaled. "I'm not sure of the word for it."

"Ah, I understand. Easy solution." He used a pen to mark a big X on my firm's brochure. "I say no to proposal. So, I'm not client. No more problem." He smiled, "So, dinner?"

I pointed to the brochure. "I think you should reconsider my proposal."

He glanced at it and shrugged. "I have friends in other companies. I help you get them as client. I promise. Dinner?"

"Wait. This is . . . unexpected. I don't know anything about you."

"What you want to know? Ask."

"Erm . . . your first name."

He smiled. "Apostol."

"Apostle? Like the title?"

He chuckled as he spelled it. "Mean same thing. But is my name. Next question."

"I don't know. Don't you have a wife or girlfriend or something?"

"No."

"Why?"

His eyes smiled. "I tell you at dinner."

At that moment, I remembered my Iya Agba's saying about finding what you've searched for in faraway Sokoto, right there in your shokoto.

Week 12

My doorbell rang.

As I walked to the door, I glanced at my watch and thought that Pastor (as I now called Apostol) was early. He was supposed to pick me, we drive to Marina, and take a boat to a private beach near Tarkwa Bay. I opened the door.

A man said, "Hello, Ohemaa."

I smiled as we hugged. Kwesi, my Ghanaian friend, was the only person who called me Ohemaa. As we unclasped from the hug, he said, "You're still Ghanaian Black."

"You still look like a wannabe Majid Michel." Because I was darker, and he was biracial, we always had silly running jokes about our complexions.

"What?" He chuckled. "You're still crazy."

"Ah! Don't swear for me abeg. I'm not crazy in Jesus name." I took a step back and waved him in. "Come in. This is a pleasant surprise."

He came in, looked around my living room. "You've done up your place. It was nice before, but it's great now. I like it. Especially how airy it is."

"Thanks. It's been awhile since you were here."

He sat on a couch, but I knew he wasn't going to sit for

long. Kwesi was naturally restless. "Yeah. The last time we saw was two years ago."

"That long? Life, eh? You didn't tell me you were coming to Nigeria."

"How could I? You don't take my calls."

"But we text naw. You know I've been busy."

"Liar. It's because of my wife."

I chuckled. "Yes, that too. You know how it can be with wives and female friends. I have to respect her and keep boundaries. So, how've you been, Chale? You want something to drink? Your choices are water, Sprite, and zobo."

He got off the couch and began to pace the room. "You know I don't like you calling me that. It makes me feel I'm just your friend. Like I've been friend-zoned."

I smiled. "Chale, you're just my friend. And you were always friend-zoned."

"I'm working on changing that, Ohemaa. Since we met, I've always been working on that."

"Who sent you this hopeless work?"

We'd met twelve years ago, as the only Black people in our undergraduate class at the University of Dundee. We hung out, faced the cold and culture together, ate and bantered, and eventually became friends. But we bonded when my Iya Agba died in my final year.

I was born in London to Nigerian parents. My mother, who never recovered from a rare case of postpartum preeclampsia after giving birth to me, died when I was two. My father raised me as a single dad as best he could until he died from a sudden stroke during our visit to Nigeria when I was ten. That's how his mother, my Iya Agba, a semiliterate but resourceful trader in Balogun Market, raised me. She was a formidable woman who made sure I never lacked, taught me Yoruba, how to negotiate and sell, and how to face life with equanimity and humor. When I got the news of her death, Kwesi was an unexpected rock. In the weeks and months that followed, he held me when I wailed, made sure I ate, cleaned my room, did my laundry, traveled down to Nigeria with me for the funeral, did my coursework, and made his family stand in for mine during our graduation.

He laughed. "The only reason why we didn't date in Dundee was because it was never the right time. We were always with other people."

"You mean you were always with girls?"

"They were always with me!"

"Liar! But you were never my type sha. You know I always preferred older men."

"That's what you always say. But I'll quote Speed Darlington in that video and say—Try me. Take risk and succeed."

I guffawed. "What? Are you mad, Kwesi? Where's your wife?"

He stopped smiling. "She's in Accra." His eyes darkened. "We're getting divorced."

I went silent. Then I sighed. "What did you do?"

"Why do you think it was my fault?"

"Because I know you. You have ojukokoro-eye for every woman. Now, what did you do?"

"It doesn't matter. We're getting divorced. That's why I came to Lagos. To tell you. I want us to be together after the divorce. You know we'll be good together."

"Omo ase! Are you mad? I've got a boyfriend. You know I'm big on boundaries."

"Who's he?"

"Pastor. He's Ukrainian." I smiled. "He's also my client."

He raised an eyebrow. "You're dating a white man?"

I sighed. "I got tired of Lagos men. And I grew up."

"Still, I never figured you'd date a Ukrainian pastor."

I smiled. "His first name is Apostol. Yeah, it means Apostle. I nicknamed him Pastor."

He paced to the open double casement window nearest the door and sat on the edge. "Are you happy with him?"

"I'm content. He's crazy about me. Respects me, accepts my choices. He's financially comfortable. Refreshingly honest. Easy to talk to. Easy to be silent with. Sex is good enough. No drama. Proper grown-up relationship. Yes, he ticks most of my boxes."

"He's much older, I guess."

I smiled. "Of course. He's fifty-one."

Years ago, Kwesi had remarked that I preferred older men because subconsciously I was looking for a father figure to replace my late father. He also said I didn't fancy marriage or serious relationships because, after the losses I'd suffered, I feared committing to people. I'd told him to fuck off.

"You love him?"

"Love isn't always necessary, Chale."

He sighed. "Ohemaa, you know I love you, right?"

"Abeg. Abeg. You're worse than all the Lagos men I know combined."

My doorbell rang.

Pastor stood at the door.

I hailed him as usual. "My Pastor." I leaned in for a kiss, but noticed he kept his face like he was smelling spoilt ewa. He pushed me gently and made his way inside the house. It was unnecessary because I was about to invite him in.

"What going on? Who this?"

"Meet my friend, Kwesi. Kwesi, meet my boyfriend, Apostol." Kwesi stood and offered his hand.

Apostol ignored it, turned, and glared at me. "Your friend I don't know?" I'd never seen this side of Pastor before.

"What? You don't know all my friends."

"Yes. But I hear this friend say he love you. Just now, eh?"

Kwesi put his hands up placatingly. "Look, man, I'm—"

Pastor cut him off. "No! No talk."

I sighed. "Listen, Kwesi is one of my dearest friends. I can't forget or repay him for what he has done for me. Yes, occasionally, he says he loves me. But it's just that—words. Nothing has happened between us, and nothing will happen."

Pastor spat his words with clipped tones. "You have good man now." He poked his chest. "Me! You too old to change man every day. So, you never talk to . . ." he pointed to Kwesi ". . . that man again. Okay?"

And just like that, time slowed. And stood still.

See ehn, in this life, you need to know yourself. I know myself. I like to joke and talk nonsense, but I will disgrace myself and my Iya Agba kpata-kpata, if I allow one more man stand on top my head in this Lagos.

"Get out," I whispered.

He was surprised. "What?"

I pointed to the door. "Get the fuck out of my house, Mr. Zherdev."

I caught a glimpse of a smile on Kwesi's face, and I turned to him. "And you. You and I will never be together. I need you, as my friend, to respect that and keep the needed boundaries."

Week 13

I'm no longer with Pastor.

Susan said Kwesi is back with his wife. She told me because I had no way of knowing. After that day, he blocked me on all social media platforms. I don't know why, and frankly, I no longer care.

And I've gotten over oyibo men in Lagos.

Looking back though, sometimes I wonder if there is a peculiar madness that possesses men once they are in Lagos? Are all men in Lagos mad or is it me?

In the end, I'm back where I started—still tired of Lagos men. Nearly all of them are mad. Awon weyrey!

ỌDẸ-PUS COMPLEX

"Young lady, please, I need you to exchange seats with my son," said the woman sitting beside Jide on the plane.

Jide was listening to Burna Boy's new song, so she wasn't sure she heard right. The woman tapped her lightly and she took off her earpiece.

"Ma?"

"Please, can you exchange seats with my son?" She was graying, matronly, and Ankara-clad. She turned around as she pointed backward to her son. Jide turned to look at him. He was seated a row behind, on the other side of the aisle. The plane's layout was three seats on each side with an aisle in the middle. Jide had come to the airport and checked in early because she wanted to ensure she got her preferred aisle seat, and she had. The older woman was in the middle, while another lady took the window seat. Now she was being asked to swap seats with someone on the other side with a middle seat.

Jide hated middle seats on planes.

But she had a soft spot for tall, bearded men with thick brows and shy smiles—which was exactly what the son was. She'd noticed him when she'd got on the plane (as usual, she'd got on last because she preferred if everyone had settled in, as she couldn't stand the preflight bedlam of people struggling with overhead lockers and seat belts).

Now he smiled at her as he noticed she and his mother appeared to be talking about him. The woman explained, "I'm an old woman and I need his help on flights."

Jide figured that the woman was probably scared of flying. Besides, the flight was a short one, the fifty-minute hop from Port Harcourt to Lagos. Reluctantly, she unclasped the seat belt, stood, and walked to him. He watched her approach with a half-smile.

"Excuse me. Your mum wants us to swap seats."

He blew his cheeks and smiled apologetically. "Are you sure you're okay with this? Because . . ." His voice was deep-melodious, and he drawled.

She smiled. "It's okay. Really."

"Uchenna!" the woman called and beckoned to him.

The man stood. He was taller than she imagined. As they brushed past each other in the aisle, she inhaled his heady perfume. She stumbled. He put a strong hand on her shoulder, steadied her. He whispered, "Sorry." For his mother. For the stumble.

She found herself looking up at him and smiling. "Thanks." She relaxed into his seat, continued playing Burna Boy, and hoped the music would make her forget the usual thing that irked her whenever she flew from Port Harcourt.

It was the recurring argument with her parents, one they'd had even today when they dropped her at the airport. Originally from Lagos, her parents had found jobs and built careers as consultants and university lecturers in Port Harcourt. They'd done well enough for themselves and made friends who could get her a cushy job in any of the oil companies. So they couldn't understand why she, their only child, chose instead to slum it at some low-paying job in stressful and faraway Lagos. It irked her that despite sending him links to everything of hers that was published, her father pretended to forget that she was a staff writer at a culture and arts magazine and her freelance writing had given her bylines in *The Guardian*, the BBC, and *The New Yorker*. She knew he'd never quite forgiven her for abandoning her geology degree to, as he always described it, gallivant as a writer.

Fortunately, a combination of Burna's music and frequent glances at the bearded man's profile made her temporarily forget her parents. When the plane landed in Lagos, and they disembarked, she breezed past the man and his mother. But they caught up with her at the baggage-claim area as she waited for her luggage.

He stood next to her. "Thanks again."

"You're welcome."

"My name is . . ."

"Uchenna. I overheard."

"Call me Uche. What's your name?"

"Yejide. Everyone calls me Jide."

"Isn't Jide a man's name?"

"Yes. That's why I prefer it." She didn't explain that in her line of work, an assumed man's name gave her some type of anonymity when she wanted it, and some male privilege to reach a wider audience. Her bag trundled toward her, and she leaned forward, braced for it. He was faster though, hoisted it easily off the carousel and handed it to her.

"Thanks." She smiled and made to leave.

"You're welcome." He slipped her his card. She glanced at it. Uche Umeh. CEO, Umeh Group of Companies. "Call me."

"We need to hurry, Uchenna," his mother called out.

"Mummy, I'm thanking the lovely young lady who gave up her seat."

His mother raised a brow. "Thank you. You have not left?"

"You are welcome, ma. I'm about leaving."

"Got a car?" he asked.

"I'll take a taxi."

"Do you mind if we drop you off? Our driver is waiting outside, and the car is big enough. Where are you headed?"

"Home. Ikeja." Home was the apartment she shared with Azuka, her flatmate.

"Oh, cool. Surulere for us."

"I live on Adeniyi Jones. It's off your way."

"It's okay. Really."

Jide smiled and shook her head. "Don't worry. I'll take a taxi."

"Okay, let me walk you out."

"Your luggage."

"Don't worry about it." He beckoned to one of the airport porters, who came to him with a luggage trolley. He pointed the man to his mother. "Mummy, he will help with the bags. I'm coming." Then he turned to Jide. "Let's go."

He took her bag, rolled it behind him as they walked out into the sunshine together. Outside, a gaggle of taxi drivers called out to them, but as if he knew who she would have chosen, he signaled to an elderly man, confirmed that his AC was working, asked for how much to Adeniyi Jones, paid, and put her bag in the boot. He opened the back door for her.

"Thanks," she said.

"I should thank you instead, for what you did for my mum."

"Let's say we're even."

He smiled. "No. We'll be even when you call me."

Although she found herself thinking about him, she allowed herself to be distracted with work. Finally, she called on the fourth day, as work was winding down.

"Hello." His voice was deeper on the phone.

"This is Jide."

"Finally! I was beginning to think my mum chased you away."

"Oh no. I've been a bit busy."

"Well, I'm glad you called. What have you been up to?"

"Nothing much. Just work."

"Where do you work?"

She told him.

"That's nice. My elder sisters read your magazine. Do you write?"

"I do. Or rather, I did. I was a staff writer for three years. Got promoted to features editor on Monday, which means I won't write as much."

"Congratulations. Let me take you to lunch tomorrow to celebrate."

"Thanks, but I can't. I don't do lunch."

"Beefing with lunch?"

Jide chuckled. "No, the workload here is heavy. Nobody takes a lunch break. The best we do is eat at our desks in ten or fifteen minutes and it's back to work."

"I see. Coincidentally, I'm on the Island, and close by your office. When do you get off work?"

"In about an hour."

"If you're not driving, can I give you a ride home?"

Unlike the last time she declined his offer for a ride, at the airport, it was different now. She didn't have a car, and it would take her about a year to finish saving for one, so she had to accept safe freebies whenever she got them. Since she started work, to save on taxi and Uber costs, she carpooled with Miriam, one of her colleagues, who drove the daily Mainland-Island-Mainland shuttle. Three other colleagues also joined Miriam, and because she was the youngest, she was made to sit at the back of the car, in the middle, next to Tijan. This wouldn't have been a problem but for Tijan's suffocating Arabic perfume, which choked her all through the journey (which was a shame because he was such a pleasant colleague).

Still, she tried a weak attempt at a no. "I live at Ikeja. I recall you mentioned you stay at Surulere? It's too much trouble for you."

"Allow me judge my own trouble."

She smiled. "Okay, then."

"One more thing. Can I bring you anything to eat when I come for you?"

"Don't worry about it."

He called when he got to her office, and when she came out, he stood outside in the car park and waved. "In case you'd forgotten what I look like," he joked. His dark T-shirt put a spotlight on his wide shoulders and athletic frame. His eyes were softer and his smiles shyer than she remembered, and it was a turn-on that he was oblivious of how gorgeous he was. She offered her hand for an awkward handshake when she really wanted to hug him.

They got in his SUV, and he offered to take her to a lounge to get some food as she hadn't eaten lunch, but she declined. When he stopped at Glover Court to pick up pre-ordered suya for his mother (a habit of his, anytime he was on the Island, he explained), he persisted gently again, and she agreed to some takeaway suya. They got cold drinks from roadside hawkers and sipped as he drove. It was easily her most enjoyable ride in Lagos traffic. He was excellent company, easy to talk to, and he made her laugh effortlessly. She loved the soft, soothing rumbles of his laughter; and enjoyed the gentle flexes of his biceps as he drove smoothly with one hand. He smiled like a dream when he caught her stealing glances at him, which was often.

She didn't want the ride to end. So she was pleased that when they got to her house, he parked outside, and they stayed in the car talking. She could have invited him in, but Azuka was home. They talked till it got late, and she sighed and said, "I've got to go. I have to be at work by six in the morning."

"I'd like to see you again sometime soon."

"Okay. What do you have in mind?"

"I've got some business on the Island for this week and next. How about I pick you up from work every day for the rest of this week, and the whole of next week?" He smiled. "We get to do this every day. What do you say?"

She couldn't pass up the chance to not smell Tijan's perfume. So she agreed. And in the time they spent together in car rides and outside her house in the following days, she learned more about him.

He was the only son and the youngest of three children. His father died when he was young, and his mother took over the running of his father's auto parts business because she regarded it as his inheritance to be protected till he became a man. From when he was a child, he'd worked in the business during school holidays. Now he ran the businesses because his mother claimed to be retired. Despite her claim, she remained the de facto CEO of the group.

The most important thing she learned, though, was that he was single. She could also see that he liked her, and she expected him to make quicker moves, but he took what she considered a long time.

When he dropped her home on the Wednesday of the following week after their first ride, he unhooked his seat belt, leaned across, and kissed her just before she opened the door. Stunned by the force of the pleasure waves, she clung tightly to him. She exhaled when they stopped and he whispered, "That was intense. We're going to be dynamite in bed." She wanted more but he said, "Good night, Jide."

He picked her from work on Thursday and Friday. They talked and joked about everything but the kiss. And he didn't touch her. She was disappointed but tried not to show it.

On Sunday, when she didn't expect to see him, he called.

"Are you home?"

"Yes."

"Did Azuka travel yesterday like you said she'd planned?"

"Yes. Why?"

"I'm at your door."

She flew out of bed and opened the door. And there he was, smiling.

"I tried to fight the sudden and inexplicable need to see you, but I failed. So, I'm here. Are you alone?"

She smiled. "Yes."

"Good."

He kissed her. She pulled him in from the doorway, and as he entered, he closed the door with his foot. They kissed till they had to come up for air.

"I've wanted to do that again since the last time, but I held back."

"Why?"

"I like you and don't want you to doubt my feelings. So, first, I'm going to ask—will you be my girlfriend?"

She chuckled. "You're so formal. Oya now, bring a contract for me to sign yes."

He beamed. "Cool. So, is it okay if we make love now or do you want to wait?"

"Are you mad? Fuck me before I change my mind."

"Say please."

She flung her arms around his neck as they resumed the frenzied kissing. When he backed her against the wall, she pulled her tank top over her breasts, then unbuttoned her tight bum shorts and pushed them down after a quick shake of her hips. He had masterful hands—one hand fondled her breasts and nipples skilfully like he already knew them; while his other hand between her legs had two fingers tapping and stroking her G-spot, and the heel of his hand pressed-caressed her clitoris.

She struggled to stand, so he turned her, pushed her to the couch, and bent her over the back of the couch. She was still on her feet, but her face and torso rested on the seat. He knelt behind her, spread her buttocks, slipped a finger back in to massage her G-spot, and stuck his lips and tongue between her legs. He kept at it, moan-growling softly, till her toes curled, and pressure built, and a small bomb of bright electric tingles went off through her body, and the wetness trickled down her shaking legs, and she squealed through her orgasm.

Then she reached behind her, grabbed his penis, lifted one leg slightly, and guided it inside her. He managed a few strokes before he said, "Your pussy squeeze kills me. I'm going to cum." Quickly, she pushed him out, spun, and got on her knees. "Cum in my mouth," she said, as she tugged him to her face, but he groaned and burst in her fingers. She still took him in her mouth though, and sucked till his knees buckled and he sank on the rug beside her.

They lay in silence, her arm across his thigh, his limp penis still in her hand, and his jeans bunched up at his ankles. Her eyes were closed when she said, "You were right."

"About what?"

"We're dynamite in bed."

"Technically, we haven't gotten to the bed yet."

"We're going there next."

"You still haven't said please."

They'd dated for three months before she realized she'd never been to his house. When she looked back, she wondered if she'd been distracted by the thrill of always-great sex—in his car, at her place, a hotel, and his friend's house.

"I just realized I don't know where you live."

"You never asked, babe."

"I didn't realize I had to ask."

There was an awkward silence during which he looked away. Eventually, he said, "I stay in the same compound with my mum."

"You stay with your mum?"

"No. We stay in the same compound but in different houses. She stays in the house in front, I'm in the one at the back."

"Hmm. Interesting."

"You know what? I'll take you to meet her this Sunday. It's important she likes you."

"Hmm. Are you sure about this?"

He smiled. "Don't worry, babe."

On that Sunday, she wore a knee-length Ankara shirtdress instead of the pants or jeans she typically wore. When he picked her up, he said, "Wow! You're so beautiful. This looks good on you."

She understood what he meant when he said they lived in separate houses. The big compound housed a detached duplex in front and a bungalow at the back, which he explained used to be the BQ till it was converted to a two-bedroom apartment for him. He took her first to the duplex. As they waited for his mother to join them, she stared at the too-ornate furnishings and old framed pictures of his father (to whom Uche bore an uncanny resemblance).

As his mother came down the stairs, Jide smiled and knelt in greeting. "Good afternoon, ma."

She replied with a plastic smile and nod.

"Mummy, this is Jide."

She nodded again. "Thank you for coming. You're the one I asked for a seat on the plane?"

"Yes, ma."

"Who knew you'd now want a seat in our family?" She chuckled but it didn't get to her eyes.

"You're so funny, Mummy." Uche's laugh suddenly sounded weird. "Jide is a geologist."

Jide smiled. "I left geology three years ago, ma. I'm a writer."

Uche gave his weird laugh again. "But you're still a trained geologist."

She wasn't sure what he meant, so she nodded.

The woman sized her up. "Jide." Yorubas and Igbos both had Jide as a given name but pronounced differently. Jide couldn't help but notice his mother had used the Igbo pronunciation of her name.

"Yes, ma."

"Who are your parents?"

"They're both university professors, ma. My dad teaches geology, and my mum, petrochemical engineering."

"That's not what I meant. I mean, I'm sure they taught you better than to wear something this short, with that slit, to come and see me. As I was coming down and you were sitting in the chair, I could see everything you have." She smiled but it had no warmth. "But you're young, and maybe this is today's fashion, and maybe Uchenna didn't tell you my expectations." She turned to him. "Uchenna, is it good what your girlfriend is wearing?"

He tried to play it off. "Ah, Mummy."

"Answer me."

His smile was sheepish. "I see your point, Mummy. It's not too good like that."

Her smile was triumphant. "Thank you. Now, come, let's go and eat." Then, almost like an afterthought, she added, "You too, Jide."

She led the way to the adjoining dining room, where Jide wasn't surprised to see a full spread laid out on a rococo-style dining table. "Uchenna, I also prepared your favorite oha soup if you want some. I hope Jide knows how to make it?"

"I don't, ma, but I'm willing to learn. Will you teach me?"

She smiled. "I don't share my recipes. Ask your mother or use YouTube."

They ate lunch while being waited on by two lady-helps. And though the food was delicious, Jide picked her food because she was stewing. It turned bitter when, sometime during the meal, his mother leaned back, dabbed her lip with a napkin, and said, "I hope Uchenna has told you about his fiancée, Adaobi?"

They had their first fight immediately after they left his house.

Still sensitive about her parents' reaction to her writing, first she accused him of also being ashamed she was a writer because he'd tried to impress his mother instead with her geology degree. He admitted though that he didn't want to talk about her writing because she hadn't completed her novel-in-progress, and it was almost impossible for many older Nigerians to take unpublished writers seriously, when they barely acknowledged published ones (and no, her online articles and stories wouldn't count as publication for his mother). She didn't take it well.

Then she talked about the many subtle and obvious ways his mother put her down and how he didn't protect her. He said his mother hadn't put her down, and she was overreacting, and she should calm down. And she absolutely did not calm down.

Finally, there was Adaobi. He explained that Adaobi was a girl his mother had wanted him to marry, especially as they were both from Nnewi, and her father, a transport magnate, and his late father had been friends. He admitted that they'd dated briefly, and while he'd never proposed, both families had taken to treating them like they were engaged. They'd broken up partly because there was little attraction between them, and because they'd quickly realized their relationship was more of a potential business merger to their families. His mother had refused to accept the breakup.

They were still fighting in the car when he got to her

house. There was no usual goodbye kiss when she came down. They didn't speak the next day, a Monday. He called on Tuesday, but she didn't take his call. Instead, she sent him a text saying she needed some time to think, and she'd contact him. On Thursday, she got a text from an unknown number: *This is Mrs. Umeh. We need to talk. Come and see me.*

Out of respect, she called Mrs. Umeh, who was polite on the phone, and scheduled to see her on Saturday morning. On Saturday, she dressed purposely in an off-shoulder short romper, which was shorter than what she wore at their first meeting, and took an Uber to the house. She didn't see Uche's car in the compound. The staff let her in the living room, and his mother came downstairs almost immediately.

Her face was inscrutable when she saw Jide's outfit, but Jide hoped she got the message. She pointed to two high-backed chairs, facing each other in a corner. "Sit down, Jide." This time, she pronounced her name properly. "Let's talk, woman to woman. And I will speak honestly because, in my experience, anything else is a waste of everybody's time. Besides, I'm old and I've earned the right to say whatever I want."

Jide couldn't help but smile.

When they'd settled into the seats and locked eyes, she said, "So, you reported me to my son. You said I don't like you, and I was tribalistic to you because you're not Igbo."

"I didn't report you, ma. I only said how I felt. Like you, I believe in speaking honestly."

It was her turn to smile. "Good. It is not that I don't like you. Ordinarily, I'd be indifferent to you, but you're with Uchenna, so I'm forced to have an opinion." She shrugged. "My opinion is, I don't think you're the right fit for him. And it's not any fault of yours. Let me explain by telling you a story."

She pointed to a framed almost-life-sized photograph of Uche's father, leaning on a small stretch of wall. "We met here in Lagos, but came from similar backgrounds—we had both lost our entire families and had been orphaned by the Biafran War, at a time we were old enough to never forget. We got married in Lagos. Together, we struggled at first, but slowly, we built a life, even bought this house. He sold auto parts from his shop at Ladipo, I was a schoolteacher.

"Then Nigeria killed him. Nineteen ninety-two. Some students were protesting the military government. Some soldiers came and started shooting. My husband, going about his business, caught a stray bullet. In the typical Nigerian way, nobody apologized, and nobody was brought to justice.

"Uchenna, our only son, was two. In our culture, bloodlines, legacies, and inheritances are fundamental to who a man is. So it became my duty to raise a son whose entire paternal lineage had been wiped out, and provide him with some sort of legacy and inheritance."

She shrugged. "The inheritance was the easy part. I resigned as a teacher and ran the business. I grew it from one shop in Ladipo to four shops nationwide: in Onitsha Main Market, Asa-Nnentu in Aba, and Abuja. I diversified to high-end auto-repair workshops in Lagos and Abuja. And during Uchenna's university days in America, we started our auto dealership arm, with him buying the cars and shipping to Nigeria for us to clear and sell. I've done my duty and handed over the businesses to him. His inheritance is secure.

"Bloodlines and legacies are trickier, no? I couldn't resurrect the dead. But I did little things. I filled this house with his father's pictures. I talked to him about his father a lot. And I tried to convince him to marry from his father's people. That's why I prefer Adaobi. Uchenna thinks it's simply because of her father's money, but he's mistaken.

"Perhaps, now you'll understand why I said, through no fault of yours, I don't think you are a good fit for my son. You can disagree and call it tribalism, and you may be right to an extent, but honestly, I don't care about your opinion. Your experiences may have given you the privilege to be detribalized. Not mine. I've seen war, and too many deaths, and I understand what Nigeria really is."

She exhaled. "I can do many things, but I cannot force a wife on Uchenna. He told me he loves you. That means I have to, at least, tolerate you and treat you respectfully. I as-

91

sume this will be reciprocated, but I'm indifferent if it isn't." She signaled at Jide's outfit. "I can see you're a fighter, and strong-willed. Even though we'll disagree on many things, I think those are good traits for you to have as a woman in Nigeria. Who knows if we may end up liking each other someday?"

For a moment, they stared at each other. "Uchenna has asked for permission, and I have given him permission to marry you."

"Permission?"

"Yes," she deadpanned. "But there are two conditions. The first is, you must get pregnant before the wedding. We need to be sure you're fertile. We have a legacy to protect and a lineage to rebuild. The second is, you will both live here after the wedding because it is his father's house. Don't worry, I can move into the apartment at the back, while he moves here so there will be enough space for you and your children. We can also renovate and redecorate any way you want, though of course, you understand that most of his father's pictures and things will have to remain as they are, right?"

"Hey, babe."

Uche came into the living room as she was speaking. She

hadn't seen him in a week, and it almost felt like she was seeing him again for the first time. It re-surprised her how perfect he was—the full and coiffed beard, shy and boyish smile, mischievous eyes, and toned biceps peeking from under rolled T-shirt sleeves. And her heart ached so much, she blurted, "Hey, babe. I've missed you so much."

His uncertain smile turned into his familiar happy laugh. She jumped in his arms, hung on his neck, buried her face in his shoulder, and sobbed quietly. "I'm so sorry, Uche. I love you. I'm so sorry. I love you."

Surprised, he held her, rubbed her back gently, and cooed, "I love you too, babe," while looking at his mother like what-amazing-thing-did-you-do. And his mother shrugged.

Jide stepped back but held his face in her hands and just stared at him. He pulled a handkerchief and dabbed her tears gently, careful not to smudge her makeup. Eventually, she pulled herself from his arms and turned to his mother.

"I'm sorry, ma . . . for the scene."

Mrs. Umeh shrugged.

"Thank you for speaking honestly. I understand everything now, and I respect you so much for how you have overcome every adversity and raised your son."

Mrs. Umeh nodded.

"But now I agree with you on one thing—I'm not the right fit for Uche."

A faint smile appeared on Mrs. Umeh's face, and she nodded again: in thanks, in respect, or both, Jide wasn't sure.

As Uche's face fell, she hopped and pecked his cheek. "I love you, Uche, but I'm so sorry. I can't do this anymore. Sorry. Bye." Then, in a flash, she was at the door, and out of the house.

He called out to her, but she kept running.

A LOVER'S VENDETTA

If we ever meet again, only one of us will leave the encounter unharmed. If I don't kill you, I will leave a mark so deep and prominent on your body, people will cross the road for you. Anybody with sense will look at the mark and know that only a worthless person will do something deserving of such a scar. They will be as pitiless with you as you were with me for four years, Dele. The anger that has been boiling my blood since the year you disappeared will never be cooled until I inflict the same pain on you.

We met when we were both trying to find our paths in life. You were a twenty-seven-year-old mechanic at John Holt and I was twenty-five years old. We sat side by side on the BRT bus from Jibowu to Abule Egba. I was so tired from working that day at my cleaning job in General Hospital, Sabo, that I fell asleep on your shoulder. Maybe for other people my job would have been something shameful. But I can never be ashamed of making my own money. When the ATM brings out naira notes, they look the same no matter how you have earned it.

Besides, cleaning people's messes at the clinic was perhaps one of the most therapeutic phases of my life. Do you know why? Because everyone takes a shit in the toilet once they receive bad news. When I clean up their mess, it's almost like I am helping their life make sense again. Shit business is serious business o, Otunba Gadaffi said so. And that day I fell asleep on your shoulder was one of those days I did major cleaning at the hospital.

There was a girl who vomited her fears on the ground, missing the toilet by a foot, after the doctor told her she was unable to have a child because she had aborted too many times and no life wanted to germinate in her anymore. Then there was the man who held his son as the doctor told them they had to amputate his left leg, who now went into the toilet and messed it up. He cried for his son who had not started living, yet had to let his leg go. I kept the toilets sparkling all day so that people like the pregnant woman and her potbellied ex-husband could comfortably use it as a place to argue, to once again reaffirm the reason why they didn't need to be together anymore.

Everyone always leaves a mess in the hospital's toilets. I did not mind it at all, I found cleaning soothing. It was not the worst job I ever had and I didn't look down on myself. I knew I was going to make it in life so I was okay with the many phases and curveballs life threw at me.

That day after my shift, I may have drooled as I dozed off on your shoulder. I tend to drool and snore when I am exhausted. Dele, it was tiredness that led me to you. I leaned on you, trusted you before I even knew you. I should have chosen the other empty seat beside the woman who had a basket of stockfish on her lap. I just didn't want to spend hours in traffic inhaling the sweet smell of fish mingled with the other smells that filled the BRT. So I chose to sit beside the young man with the clean white shirt. Anyone who could keep a white shirt clean at the end of the day in Lagos deserved a standing ovation. But I should have known that any man who could keep a clean white shirt at the end of a Lagos workday would be dangerous.

If I had chosen to sit beside the other woman, perhaps our journeys would have been different. Maybe another woman could have dealt with you.

"Excuse me, I think we are in Abule Egba. I hope we have not gone past your bus stop," you had whispered gently in my ears so that you didn't bring me from my dreams abruptly.

I woke up and looked at you. I took a breath in, hoping to catch your smell, but nothing met my nose except the stench that came from the wig of the lady sitting in front of us. I know the smell was from her because I had bumped into her as we struggled to get onto the bus.

This is why I keep a low-cut. I don't understand why women punish themselves using wigs. This is a hot country and you don't have car with AC. Me, I don't like that kind of stress.

"I am sorry, I didn't know when I slept off."

"It's okay, I could tell you were tired."

I wanted to tell you a little bit about my day but my thoughts were cut short by the driver, who honked all of us out of the bus.

"We don reach na. Make una comot. Passengers dey wait abeg."

We all rushed to get off, but as we clambered down, I noticed you held my hands to keep me safe.

"I'm Dele," you said after we finally got out of the chaos.

"Nice to meet you. My name is Orode."

"Orode?"

"Yes."

"That is a beautiful name."

You walked me to the spot under the bridge to take an okada home. Even though I was tired, we still talked for another thirty minutes. We gisted like old friends. We had a lot of things in common but the deepest bond we shared was the loss of both our parents.

That night when I got home, I told Chuchu that I had found my husband.

A year after we met on the bus, we were married. I had gotten a job as an Uber driver and I was making money, you were on the rise as a mechanic in John Holt, so we moved from Abule Egba to Salvation Road in Opebi. The morning of our registry wedding, Chuchu adjusted the strap of my bra, pulled the neckline of my oversized wedding dress, and asked why I chose to marry you.

"What about Ebuka? That man really loves you."

"Chuchu, please focus on your boyfriend of four years that has given you a ring but won't walk you down the aisle," I said. It was easier to deflect than try to defend my decision because I knew she wouldn't understand.

Yes, Ebuka loved me, but there is love and then there is love. You see, Ebuka's own reminded me of when my mother was alive and we were still living in our unpainted house in Warri. She used to buy these small, small ceramic things, like ducks and cats, and arrange them in one cupboard that had glass covering. The roofing sheets of our house used to shake and vibrate with any small breeze and when it rained nko? We used to sweep water out every morning from April to September. But those her ceramic toys were her pride and joy. She would polish them on Sunday mornings, humming and singing to herself in our parlor. To Ebuka, I was one of those toys. If I stay with him, our cement house will be flooded with water, but he will be petting me, thinking that he is happy and content.

You see your own, Dele, you were the kind that if there is a riot, tear gas full everywhere and sirens are sounding off, I believed that you would come and find me. You would hold my hand and you would run with me to find safety. In the life I saw for myself, the way I saw you, you were the husband for me. The love that I needed. With your charm and looks, you could have gotten anyone else but you chose me. I didn't believe that a prince was going to come riding into Abule Egba on a white horse to save me and carry me off to Ikoyi. You were the closest to a Prince Charming for me, and I was content.

"My dear, no vex. I will leave you be. Marry him. I will support you," Chuchu conceded.

And she did just that. At the registry in Ikoyi, she followed me around with a hand-held plastic fan so that my makeup would not smudge and the wedding photographs would look nice. When I moved out of our shared room, she followed me in the rickety yellow-and-black taxi, cardboard boxes on her lap, joking about how she would be the one to do my omugwo because I had no mother and neither did Dele. Chuchu will always have my heart for standing with me.

After four months as an Uber and Taxify driver, our finances improved, even though I was splitting my profits sixty-forty with the owner of the car. It belonged to a former colleague from the hospital who wanted to help out. While she was working long hours as a doctor, her Toyota Camry was making money for both of us.

Being a driver was not dangerous at all. Like with all things, I applied sense to it. I never drove at night, preferring to start at the crack of dawn. I used to find plenty customers going to and coming from the airport, and those were lucrative trips for me. Not only that, I avoided clubs and hotels, those ones were too risky, whether night or day. I was quick to cancel those kinds of trips. In actual fact, driving Uber was very good for me as a woman because men loved to help me out.

"I like women that are industrious. I'll pay you extra to do trips offline," many of my male customers would say.

I was never harassed. I was toasted but never harassed. I guess not every man in Lagos is unfortunate. Except you, Dele, how could you be so unfortunate? Aside from the pain I feel, I am just disappointed in you. I regret sharing my money with you. I regret sharing anything with you, Dele. We were young, in love and newly married. Living in our one-bedroom apartment, filling it with our dreams, hopes, and prayers during the day and our passionate lovemaking at night. We worked hard and came home exhausted but we were never too tired to explore our bodies.

No man had ever shown my pussy the kind of love you showed it. The way your tongue swept over my clit, the way you sucked my juices dry and then made me wet again by sucking on my nipples while you teased me with your fingers. The way you kept moving your tongue in and out of my pussy, swallowing my orgasm over and over again. Dele, your tongue has more uses than your dick. You should cut that useless piece of shit between your legs off. Your tongue is enough.

Perhaps before I kill you, I will let you ride me with your tongue one last time. One for the road. At least you will die with the taste of my vagina accompanying you to the hell you came from.

You nearly took everything away from me, Dele, and for what? Wherever you are now I hope it was worth it. Marriage to you taught me a lesson I hoped never to learn. I should have known you were up to no good when you disliked Chuchu, my only true friend, closer to me than a sister, for no good reason.

"What kind of name is Chuchu?"

"It is Chichi but she chose to change it to make it unique—baby, please leave her."

"Iyawo mi, I don't like that girl, she is weird. I don't want her coming here."

I was shocked.

You knew all about us. Like Chuchu and I, you knew the emptiness of having lost your parents at a relatively young age. Mine died in a car accident when I was ten and I ended up in St. Ann's Orphanage. Unlike me who at least once knew her parents, Chuchu was abandoned from birth and was raised completely by the nuns. Whoever left her must have been in a hurry and didn't realize there was a colony of soldier ants in the grass around. Her otherwise beautiful skin is still covered in tiny scars. Is that what you found weird? You never specified.

She was my friend from the moment we met. She protected me, shared everything she had, and lifted me from the despair of being an only child with dead parents. Even now when I look at her, I remember seeing her sitting alone in the orphanage the first day I got there, she looked as alone as I felt. Dele, would you have even met me at all if not for her? We came to this Lagos together and survived the hardships as a team. We are so close I know what she is thinking sometimes before she says anything.

Thank God I didn't listen to you, I would have been left with nothing if I did.

Chuchu might be weird but she was right about you being wrong for me. The first year we were married, it was not obvious to me. The many times your uncle would sit in our space and admonish us. You always stood up for me.

"You people should start now, so that your children will grow with you."

I'm sure I don't need to tell you that I never liked your so-called Uncle Fimihan. I tolerated him, because people like us that don't have parents collect any family we can find to represent us, so we won't suffer too much in this world without the protection we have lost. This uncle might as well have been found on the roadside, based on how useless he was, but I didn't complain about him coming over once a month to eat all the meat in my soup and imply that I was barren.

"By next year, my wife will be pregnant. Please don't put us under pressure."

"My friend, keep shut. I am the only one here since your father, my brother died. All the other relatives ran away. Until your mother succumbed to cancer, I helped train you and your brothers. I want to see my grandchildren, Dele, it's the least you owe me."

"Haba Uncle, please take it easy on my wife, she's just

twenty-six. We are not even in a hurry to end our honey-moon."

The way you defended me always got me excited. I couldn't wait for him to leave so we could be naked. I craved the sensation of your dick sliding into me, filling me up with your semen. Uncle Fimihan didn't need to beg me to carry your seed. You knew how much I loved children.

Maybe it's because I was an only child, and you were not. The fact that I did not have a close blood relation in this wretched life was the saddest thing for me. It was another reason why I married early. I was going to have at least four children. I was young, and I was working hard, saving every kobo and investing what was left. You and I opened a special account with UBA for our future children's future. I was patient, I knew it was only a matter of time before my life would be complete.

Who knew that it would all end like this?

In our second year of our marriage, my doctor friend came up with a suggestion that I refused at first.

"Orode, you are a hard worker and you are smart. More than that, you love children and you are kind. I will recommend you for nursing school. It's just three years, why not give it a try?"

I told her that it is that issue of children that won't allow me to commit to three years of schooling. I got a good enough education with the nuns at St. Ann's, and my WAEC had carried me this far. I am not a greedy person; I don't need the whole world. I would have been happy with just you and me, and our children, when they came. We had been trying for ten months by that point and there was nothing. My periods came as usual. Painful and heavy. Chuchu and I were even still having our periods together. Her time-wasting fiancé could have bought shares with Durex by that point. He didn't want to marry and he didn't want to make her a mother either. We lamented to each other. Cried and prayed together, hoping for a change in our situation.

Dele, when I told you about Dr. Ola's suggestion you surprised me by asking me to give it a try. You encouraged me by saying nursing and motherhood go together, and that having my own children will make me a better nurse and vice versa. You told me we could use some of our savings and investments to pay the fees.

That July, after some extra lessons to brush up on the core subjects, I passed the exams and was accepted into the nursing school in Alimosho. That night when you came home, I didn't even let you take off your clothes or take a shower. I pushed you into the armchair in the living room, unzipped your trousers, and gave you a blow job. Your eyes rolled back into your head as I slurped and sucked as an expression of the joy I felt that my life was finally heading somewhere.

What a fool I was.

A year went by quickly. Dr. Ola was right; it was like I was made for nursing. It was the only thing that made bearable the fact that I was still without a child of my own.

We had gone to see three different doctors and they all said we were completely fine, physically. Uncle Fimihan brought us some stinking concoctions to drink, to bathe with, and to rub on our private parts before sex. I refused to use any of it. I told you I was a professional in the medical field—taking unlicensed drugs was beneath my station in life. Another year passed, and I gave in and started using them religiously and calling your uncle for more once they finished.

We decided that it was possible that the stress of working and schooling full-time was the cause. But I had gone too far to stop. Our savings had dropped to a third of what it used to be. I told myself I had a year left and then I would be a mother. I had been patient enough; I knew God would answer my prayers. And he did, except it wasn't the one that I was expecting.

A week after our fourth wedding anniversary, I went to see Dr. Ola. She called me to share some news. When I entered her small office in her private practice in Ogba, her smile was as big as the moon. Her dark skin looked like there were lanterns underneath it. She was so happy she could have started dancing. I didn't need to ask. Unlike Chuchu's eternal fiancé, her own had not only proposed, a date had been set. Not only that, she told me, sitting me down across from her, she was pregnant.

Dele, I tried to be happy for her. And I was. Truly. I don't know why I started crying instead. Because she is a kind person, she was concerned, not angry. She had never seen me cry. I broke down and told her about our infertility journey, and how no one could tell us what the problem was. She immediately booked us for a consultation with a reproductive specialist that she knew. I was so relieved. I felt hopeful. Maybe we would finally get to the bottom of what was going on. I sent you a text with the date of the appointment and the address and went to school.

It had rained that night and NEPA had cut the light. We had just turned off our small generator because we wanted to sleep without noise. You had gone into the bedroom to spray it with insecticide. I was sitting in the living room scrolling through my phone. I never went on Facebook anymore. It was either full of bad news about the country or good news about other people celebrating the birth of their children. I was on Twitter laughing at something I don't even remember. How long were you standing there? I only remember looking up and seeing you standing before me. You were crying.

"What's wrong?" I said in a small voice as you went on your knees and buried your head in my thighs.

"Orode, I can't father a child."

"Dele, I know you're scared. I have been scared too. That all the other doctors missed something. Don't blame yourself, this new doctor will—"

"They lied. They all lied because I paid them to lie. Orode, I'm infertile. I have known since I was a teenager, but I didn't want to lose you, so I didn't tell you."

The world tilted. It was at that moment that I understood that a person can suddenly run mad. It was like I was underwater, falling and falling without reaching the bottom. Everything my eyes landed on was swimming and moving. As you told the story of how a kick in the testicles during a weekend football game with your friends damaged you for life, and how you had made several efforts to get all the women who dated you pregnant, I felt nothing. I watched you cry but all I wanted to do was smash against the wall the head that you had the audacity to leave on my lap.

You had booked all the previous doctor's appointments. Even the last one Uncle Fimihan recommended to us. It was because I was busy, you said. I thought you were so considerate, so kind.

As you begged and cried throughout the night, depriving me of sleep, the only thing I wanted to do was clean. I wanted to clean the house and rid it of you. I wish I had killed you then. You took four years away from me. Four years I could have spent loving another or even loving myself more.

The next morning your uncle showed up at the door. With my brand-new eyes I could finally see how pathetic he was. All his faded Ankara outfits and the stupid leather slippers he wore and his sad ugly toes. When his robust lips started to spew more lies, I stopped him.

"Uncle, did you know Dele cannot impregnate a woman?"

He said nothing but his eyes told me everything. This mad man sat with us, ate my food, gave us who knows what rubbish to be rubbing and drinking for children he knew would never come. I didn't say anything. I shut the door on his face on my way out.

I found Chuchu and told her everything. She went with me to the appointment, and a week after, I got the confirmation that I was physically fit to have children. On the evening of the betrayal, I came to the house we shared and met it emptied out. You and your wretched, cowardly uncle packed almost everything of value that we had both worked for and disappeared. After I cried and screamed, I picked up what was left and called Chuchu. Abandoned once again; she was all that I had left.

It's been a year, and I am once again working in the General Hospital, Sabo. This time as a nurse. I still clean up messes, people even vomit on my body sef, and I handle support during surgeries and now clean up people's blood too. What you did to me changed me, Dele, it nearly destroyed me. But I am putting the pieces of my life back together, just as I was on the day I met you on that BRT bus.

FIRST TIMES

You were sixteen the first time you had sex.

It was at a dingy motel in Bariga, manned by a reception-ist with a dirty white shirt. The room was at the end of a corridor that reeked of weed. Inside, Idris grumbled. "Can you imagine? This people don't have AC. Only fan. I paid five thousand naira for fan?"

You wondered why he was complaining about the money, when you were the one who had given it to him before you got to the motel. "It's okay," you said.

But it wasn't. It was sweltering. The room felt damp and had a stale smell. Ancient cobwebs hung from the ceil-ing, and old marks stained the sheets. When Idris took off your clothes, and laid you on the bed, you felt your skin crawl.

"Idris, wait. What if they have bedbugs?"

He paused. He'd kissed off all your lip gloss, and his lips

were shiny with tiny sparkles. "No. The owner changes the mattresses every six months."

"How do you know?"

"Shhh. Kiss me, Baby."

You kissed. His hands ran all over your body, grabbing, pawing. But your skin itched. You folded your arms. He frowned. "What's worrying you?"

It took you a moment to answer. "Promise me it won't hurt."

"I promise, Baby."

He lied.

The women in the porn videos you'd watched on Vera's phone also lied, because they pretended to always enjoy anal. Idris enjoyed himself though. You felt he was trying to prove an inexplicable and unnecessary point with his rough thrusts. He grunted. "You like that big dick, Baby?"

You didn't like it.

"Scream for me, Baby!"

You wanted to scream but you cried silently. He glanced at your tears. He didn't stop. As you lay there, you blamed your mother. Every night, she stuck her fingers between your legs in a crude virginity test. "I need to know you're pure, Ivie. Don't try me. Keep your legs closed. Avoid all these men who come here to buy things because of you. You think I don't see how they look at you?"

Your mother had a supermarket downstairs, and you helped there every day. Idris used to come to buy things from her. Then, he was tall and skinny; ridiculously handsome and he knew it. You lived in the same neighborhood and attended the same university. But he didn't notice you in school. You didn't expect him to. He was one of the popular senior guys, who all the cool and curvy girls swooned for. You were a spindly fresher with acne.

The first time he noticed you was at the supermarket and his smile gave you actual palpitations. You couldn't say no when he asked you to be his girlfriend. He asked for sex almost immediately. You held out for a month while he sulked about his needs as a man. He said he loved you. You said you loved him too, but that was a lie—you worshipped him. He said if you loved him as much as you said, you'd let him make love to you despite your mother's daily virginity tests. He hinted about going to meet someone else to satisfy his needs. Eventually, Vera, your best friend, suggested anal as a compromise so you could keep your man.

Back at the motel room, Idris said, "Call me daddy."

"Huh?"

"Call me daddy, Baby."

You didn't call him daddy. Maybe it was because you had unresolved issues with your father who left since you were two, or maybe it was the tearing pain that made it hard to talk. But you didn't want to hurt his feelings, so you whispered, "Baby. Baby. Baby." He seemed disappointed because he covered your mouth. You took the hint and went back to hmming and ahhing like they do in porn.

When he finished, there were blood streaks on the sheets, and a smell of shit in the room. You spied your clothes in a heap in a corner, and you felt silly because you'd bought a new set of clothes, down to panties, for your first time.

"Ivie, I will see you in two weeks after exams. Okay?"

You couldn't explain why you felt sad he was back to calling you Ivie, not Baby. You couldn't help but notice that the only time he had called you Baby was just before and during sex.

"Two weeks?"

He smiled. "Don't worry. I'll think about you every day."

But he stopped answering your calls after that day. He texted to say that he was busy with his exams but Vera believed that he was exasperated because you'd cried during sex. She gave you some oil to use as a lubricant and warned you against crying like a small girl.

Two weeks later, after your final exams for your first year in the university, you were ready. You planned to surprise him by spending two nights with him. You got to his BQ. The side-gate was open. As you walked in, you heard his laughter over loud music. You knocked but no one seemed to hear so you tried the door, and it opened easily. You saw Idris and a light-skinned girl kissing on his mattress. He ran his hand up her short skirt and between her thighs. Shocked, you just stared.

The girl saw you first. She stiffened, but only for a moment. She stared triumphantly at you, and pulled Idris's probing hand deeper between her legs.

Then he saw you. He almost threw her off as he scrambled to his feet. "Ivie, please. It's not what it looks like."

You couldn't see him properly because your eyes were teary.

The girl stood, walked to you with a smug smile. "Hi. I'm Belinda. But Idris calls me Baby. I'm his girlfriend."

You realized then that this was the Baby he called out for in the motel. Baby stared you down like she was daring you to do something.

You did nothing.

But you broke up with Idris. He called and texted for days, but you didn't respond. You went back home and a part of you was hurt that he didn't try to reach you there. The holidays were a blur, and the new academic year, your second year, came quickly. Your mother was still obsessed with monitoring your virginity. You needed to breathe a little, so when you were invited for a night party, you told her a lie so you could attend.

The party was at quarters, in the house of one of the popular club boys. The IV said 6, but it started at 10 p.m. The house reminded you of a coven, smoky with no furniture, with blue bulbs dancing from the ceiling. At first, you and Vera stayed glued to the wall, but the heavy weed in the air and sweet punch in your plastic cups eventually loosened you. Plus, the intoxicating music pulled you to the dance floor, where you both swayed and shimmied. You felt light for the first time in months.

Someone held your shoulders from behind and whispered softly in your ear, "Hey, stranger."

It was Idris. He danced and edged between you and Vera. Because the music was loud, he leaned in to talk to you. "Hi."

"How's Baby?" you blurted.

You were surprised that his smile still weakened you and made your heart race. He leaned in again, so you were practically necking. "We broke up that day. I'm so sorry. I miss you, Ivie. My life has not been the same without you."

As he spoke, his hand ran down your back, kissed your shoulder blades. He smelled delicious.

"I love you, Ivie. I love you so much."

You got back together that night.

You were twenty-one the first time you lost a fight.

It happened at 11:55, the club where Idris threw you a birthday party. You hadn't been keen on the party, or clubbing. At the time, your focus was on other things. You'd expected to have finished uni, but you were still in your final year due to several ASUU strikes. But you used your time well—you'd convinced your mother to open a smaller branch of her supermarket in one of the shops in the university's shopping complex, and you managed it in addition to your schoolwork. So you were always tired. Idris capitalized on this to convince you about the party. He said you needed to destress, unwind, and clubbing was perfect. You knew clubbing was his thing, but you didn't explain that it wasn't yours.

You got to 11:55 early, around 10:30 p.m. Idris's friends were already there. As always, Idris played Mr. Big Shot. They hailed him as he ordered round after round for everyone. Between rounds he'd yell, "My baby is twenty-one!" You gave him a look to stop—after his thing with Belinda, you'd asked, and he'd agreed not to call you Baby. He understood the look, but he smiled smugly and whispered, "Chill. I'm not calling you Baby. I'm telling others you're my baby. Get it?"

You didn't get it. Eventually, you ignored it and tried to get your mind into the party. You'd started enjoying yourself, when you both got into an argument. He'd ordered extra bottles of champagne, and because you were paying for all the drinks, through him of course, you were worried the extra drinks would push the bill over your budget. When you whispered your fears to him, he accused you of belittling him. He stood and walked to the direction of the restrooms. You were used to him walking off to cool off, whenever you argued. But, after you waited for an hour and he hadn't returned, you went to look for him. Some guys confirmed he wasn't in the men's restroom. You went outside. At first, you didn't see him, but you caught a slight movement from a shadowy corner. You sidled closer.

Idris leaned with his back on the wall. His eyes closed in pleasure; his zipper undone. A girl, light-skinned as usual, squatted in front of him; her skimpy dress rode up her thighs and barely covered her thick butt. Her face was set in a mask of concentration, and her jaws worked as she gave him an energetic blow job. His head was thrown back and his hands were wrapped around the bitch's hair. His mouth was open, his words inaudible, but you read his lips as he mouthed, "Yes. Yes. Yes."

You watched them till Idris's shoulders started a gentle shaking—the signal for when he was about to cum. She glanced up at him, smiled with her eyes, and seemed to will him on. You weren't going to give the bastard the pleasure of pouring his seed in her mouth.

You rushed them.

You yanked her hair, pulled her off his dick, and shoved her to the ground. You were going to beat this girl. Your confidence was based on the fact that after the incident with Belinda, you'd caught Idris with other girls (who were always light-skinned and voluptuous), and you'd learned to beat or bully all of them, so they knew not to mess with your man. This girl would be no different. She even looked fragile, and you expected an easy win as you sat on her and slapped her hard. "You like to suck other people's men, abi?"

"Ivie, please stop," Idris begged.

You turned your attention from the girl and faced him. "Useless boy! You and I are over, you hear me? Once I finish—"

You didn't see the girl start swinging. Her first blow hit your solar plexus. You felt an instant paralysis as the wind was knocked out of you. Then your body was flooded with this agonizing pain that made you slide off her. You lay on the ground in a fetal position, struggling to breathe, feeling your body spasm. She sprang on you, pinned your arms with her knees, and worked your exposed face with a flurry of punches and scratches. It happened quickly. The last thing you remember before you blacked out was the ridiculous sight of Idris, with his miserable limp penis hanging out of his jeans, trying to peel her off you.

Three hours and a shiny black eye later, Idris took you to your hostel.

"I'm sorry, Ivie. I will never do it again."

You sighed. "Why, Idris? I've done everything you've asked. Anal, vaginal, blow jobs; even started toning my skin. But you keep doing this to me. Why?"

"I'm sorry. It won't happen again."

"Fuck you! We are done."

You were twenty-eight the last time he made you cry.

You remember the day. That afternoon, Vera stopped by to see you at the Jakande branch of your supermarket. You'd grown what used to be your mother's small corner supermarket to a chain of seven mega supermarkets dotted all over Lagos. As always with Vera, she steered your conversations to men as you sat in your office while you watched the shop floor on your desktop monitor, which showed all the supermarket's CCTV cameras in real time. "I never imagined marriage would change Idris for the better. You're lucky, Ivie."

You corrected her quietly. "He changed before I married him."

That was as much gloating as you'd do. Vera smiled, shamefacedly.

She'd never forgiven him for the beating you received at 11:55. So when you took him back after he'd begged you publicly for months, she said you were making a mistake. She wasn't impressed when he put up your picture as his DP on all his social media accounts and told you all his passwords. There were no more side-chicks or one-night stands and he cut out the heavy drinking and clubbing as he'd promised—but her explanation was, he was too broke to indulge in his vices.

You disagreed. To you, Idris had matured. He became

open. Admitted his previous infidelities were driven by a mix of insecurity, pride, and immaturity. Talked about personal responsibility and growth. Dreamt of the future, with you. His honest introspection was refreshing. You grew so close, you became inseparable. For the first time in your relationship, you felt like your man's heart finally belonged to you.

You tested him. He proposed immediately you finished NYSC, but you made him wait. He was at his most loving for the two years he waited for you to say yes. You'd now been married for four years. And he'd ramped up the romance—daily calls at work, regular lunch dates during work, flowers and gifts, occasional weekend baecations at hotels. Yes, he stayed out late most nights but it was because he was working hard as a founder of three tech start-ups. Your man was yours and yours alone. Finally. No one could take him away. Vera was wrong. Your mother was wrong. You wish you could tell your mother that men value what you give them, that you'd never loved Idris as much as you did now. You wish she'd lived to see you happy with Idris, to see your life on the up. You missed your mother. It had been a year since she died from complications from her diabetes.

Vera brought you back from reminiscing about your mother. "You're inspiring me to get married o."

"Has anyone proposed?"

"Not yet."

"Ah. Okay. Have you short-listed your boyfriends?"

She chuckled. "Soon."

Later that night, you woke with a start in the dark. Immediately, you knew you had to go to the hospital. You reached across the bed but didn't feel Idris. You turned on the bedside lamp. He wasn't in the room. You got off the bed gingerly and walked to the adjoining bathroom but he wasn't there. You picked your phone. Called him. You saw his phone vibrate on his bedside table. It meant he was downstairs. You sighed. You were tired and didn't want to go downstairs twice. You put on the dress that you'd prepared for this time. You decided that Idris would have to come upstairs for the bag. You picked up your phone and a small handbag. You were ready. You walked downstairs slowly, grateful for the thick rug on the staircase that soothed your feet.

Halfway down, you heard a sound and paused, leaning on the banister.

Slower this time, you came all the way down.

The lights were off in the living room and adjoining dining room. But parts of the dining room were illuminated by slanted shafts of light from the extra-bright LED security lights from outside the house.

You saw the cause of the sound.

Idris was fucking Testimony, your house help.

They were going at it like minks. She was bent over the dining table, doggy-style, with her right leg half-raised, big buttocks perfectly arched to receive his thrusts. His pajama trousers were down to his knees. His left hand pulled and held her pink panties to her left buttock as he gripped the soft flesh. His right hand alternated between groping her heavy breasts and slapping her jiggly right buttock, leaving red handprints on her fair skin.

"Ah! Idris. Idris o," she moaned, while he made his familiar grunts.

It was the first time you'd heard her call his name. It sounded inappropriate coming from her. She usually called him oga.

You were calm as you cleared your throat, politely.

They stopped and jumped away from each other.

"Get dressed, Idris."

He stared, still frozen, confused by your lack of a reaction.

Still calm, you said, "My water just broke. The baby is coming. Get dressed. Get the bag. Take me to the hospital."

You were silent on the car ride to the hospital. You turned to the window so he wouldn't see the tears run down your face in the dark.

At the hospital he stretched a hand to hold you, but you recoiled. Because of him, you gritted your teeth and refused to groan or scream when the contractions intensified. You didn't speak to him all through the nine hours of labor. You didn't tell him when the doctors decided that it was safer to deliver the baby by cesarean section. He wanted to come into the operating theater with you, but you told the doctors you didn't want him there. After an embarrassing pause, they asked him to leave.

After your daughter was born, you told the doctors to let him in. Dead inside, you watched as he cried when he held her, your first child. It had taken you both this long to have her because of Idris's low sperm count and your inhospitable womb. The experience had bonded you both even tighter, and her birth was meant to be the biggest miracle of your love. Till he fucked it up.

So you never told him you'd instructed the doctors to tie your tubes immediately after your delivery as you still lay on the operating table.

In the recovery room, your first words to him were to say you'd named her Grace, after your mother. He opened his mouth, perhaps to remind you that you'd previously agreed to name her after his sister, but he saw the look on your face, sighed wearily, and said, "Okay." He knelt at the foot of the bed and touched your feet. "Ivie. You are my life. I promise I won't hurt you again."

You didn't say anything.

"I told Testimony to leave."

You looked at him. "Get a new dining table."

You were thirty-three when you had your first orgasm.

It wasn't from Idris. But, call it serendipity, it was Idris who introduced you to him. He was a beautiful man. Dimpled smile, white teeth, dark, bald, and walked with a slight limp. But what stood out first was his air of quiet confidence. He carried himself like a man who would be wryly unruffled by either fame or misfortune, a man who in another life would have been a king. In this life though, he was your driver, employed by your husband.

But it didn't faze him. One week after he started driving you, he said, "I like your dress. It really suits your skin tone." He said it quietly as you sat in traffic at Chevron, like it was the most natural thing in the world. You didn't know what to say, so you looked out the window and pretended not to hear him. But your face betrayed you and broke into a small smile. Your eyes met at the rearview mirror, and you knew he'd seen the smile.

Then he drew you with music. Without speaking, the man always played exactly what you needed to hear even before you knew what you needed. Like the day you were brooding because you'd found out about Idris and one of his interns, and he played this catchy tune that got your head bobbing and lifted your spirits. "What's that song?"

"'Single and Searching.' Yemi Alade and Falz."

"I like it. Play it again."

He put it on repeat as you rolled through Osapa London. "How do you always . . . ?"

You didn't finish the question, but he knew what you wanted to ask. "Uber," he answered. "I used to drive my car as an Uber until . . ." He paused. "Anyway, I learned to read people and guess the music they'd like."

"I see. What made you stop Uber?"

His jaw clenched. He spoke softly but it didn't mask the pain. "Accident. Shipping container fell off a truck. Off Ojuelegba Bridge. Crushed my car below. Killed my passenger. Almost crippled me. Took me thirteen months to learn how to walk again."

"I'm so sorry."

"Thank you. Someday, I'll be on my feet again." Then he changed the music to Rihanna's "Stay" to match the mood in the car. You spent the rest of the ride watching him—how the light from the dusk danced on his smooth ebony skin; how his strong hands gripped the wheel; and how his full lips smiled as they silently mouthed the lyrics to the playing songs. As you watched him, you couldn't understand the sudden ache in your heart.

One morning two weeks later, as you walked out from the house and entered the car, he whispered, but loud enough for you to hear, "You have an amazing figure."

You waited till your smile had gone before you said, "Listen, Ezekiel . . ."

"Call me Kel."

You exhaled. "Listen, Kel. It's not your place to talk to me like that. Don't make me report you."

"You won't."

He said it with a nonchalance, assured that you both knew it was true.

Later that night, you were working on your laptop and didn't notice when he missed the turn leading to your street. It was when he parked, you noticed you were some streets away from yours, on one of those deserted cul-de-sacs in VGC. He left the engine idling but killed the headlights. It was dark.

"Is there a problem?" Strangely, you weren't scared.

He got down and walked to your side of the car. He opened the door, leaned in, and unhooked your seat belt. You caught a whiff of his perfume, and it made you momentarily dizzy because you suddenly realized how long you'd wanted to bury your nose in his neck and smell his skin. He turned you toward him gently. The car was high, a Toyota Prado, so you were still on the back seat but facing the door, while he stood outside.

He ran a hand through your million braids. Tilted your face.

"What are you doing?" Your voice sounded choked. Your heart was beating fast.

"I'm only going to kiss you." You could hear the smile in his voice as he bent his face toward yours.

This man kissed you like it was what he was created to do. He tasted of mint, his lips were soft but had perfect pressure. He knew how to use his tongue, gently at first, then deep as you greedily drank him all in. He nibbled your lips, traced your throat with his lips, and you had to bite your lower lip to stop yourself from moaning too loudly. It felt so good. His other hand found your buttocks and he squeezed them as he pulled you against him. Through his jeans you felt his dick pushing hard between your legs. You reached down to undo his zip but he stopped you. "I'm only going to kiss you, remember?"

He pushed you gently, all the way back, so you lay on the seat. Your dress rolled up. You were embarrassed that you hadn't shaved (you and Idris no longer had sex, so you didn't care to shave). He didn't mind. As his fingers played with your hair, his thumb dipped into your wetness, stroked your clitoris. You covered your mouth with your hand to mute your moaning. Still stroking, he watched you for a long moment then whispered, "Let me taste you."

He put his head between your legs, inhaled deeply, gave you an electric lick and a moist kiss. "You smell so good." He sighed. And his words broke your heart—Idris had never gone down on you, and subconsciously, you'd wondered if you stank.

"Whatever happens, don't scream," he said against your pussy.

You nodded as he licked you with his tongue and teased you lightly with his teeth. There were ever-rising waves of pleasure as he ate you thoroughly. You felt a rush coming through. You gave yourself up as it came out of you. You blacked out.

"Ivie, wake up." He shook you gently.

He helped you sit. Your body felt weird—tingling but incredibly mellowed out. Catatonic, you watched him adjust your clothing and straighten your hair. You saw he was still hard but he simply walked to the driver's seat and drove home in silence. Your eyes were filled with sudden tears even though your heart was smiling for the first time in a long while.

You shaved that night.

The next day, you drove out in silence like nothing happened. But, instead of going to your supermarket in Oniru as planned, you told him to drive into Phase 1. You directed him down some side streets off Admiralty Way, to a secluded luxury guesthouse. You walked in alone, paid for a room, and ordered a massive breakfast tray for two. You waited for the food to be delivered before you called him. You opened the door for him, hiding behind it because you were naked. You both didn't make it to the bed until after the first feverish and magical round on the wall and the chair. It was four hours of kissing, fucking till orgasm after orgasm, eating food and each other, cuddling, a nap, and a long moment of easy silence.

It became a regular thing. Always a different guesthouse or hotel, twice a week. And it wasn't just the sex. It was everything else. He was always there. He opened doors for you, not as the driver but as a man taking care of his woman.

He always had a cold drink for you for the journey home after work. He offered to pay when you went out, which was funny since you had more money than him; but you let him. He was great with Grace and she adored him. He noticed everything about you, even when you changed your perfume. And you talked, like he was the man Idris could have been.

While cuddling one afternoon, he said in his quiet way, "I love you, Ivie. You don't have to say it back. I just want you to know how I feel." Maybe it was how he said it or the certainty in his eyes, you knew it was true. This man loved you exactly the way you'd always wanted Idris to. For a moment, you mourned for Idris and what could have been. You buried your head in Kel's chest, but didn't respond. And he held you tight. And it was enough.

That day, you knew what needed to be done. You waited for the right time to make your move. Eventually, it came, about four months later. Idris was to launch yet another start-up (though the four he had launched so far had all failed). He had scheduled a press luncheon and you were supposed to attend with him but you'd told him, at the last minute, that you'd changed your mind. He was pissed. "I made plans with you in mind. You're supposed to be there."

You shrugged and applied your makeup.

"Wait! You're not coming to the luncheon but you're going out?"

"Yes."

He looked at you suspiciously. "I thought you did your hair and nails for my event."

"Your event is not the reason why I choose to look good."

"Where are you going?"

You chuckled and waited till you finished your makeup. Then you smiled. "Pass me my phone, Idris. It's by your side of the bed."

You watched him pick the phone, which was uncharacteristically unlocked. You watched him glance at it. His face darkened. "Who the fuck is calling you Baby and why is he missing you?"

Your tone remained even. "Stop screaming like a child. Our daughter is downstairs."

He took heavy breaths, like he was gasping for air. His voice was calmer when he spoke. "Ivie, who is calling you Baby? You said you don't like being called Baby."

You shrugged. "I don't like you calling me Baby after that nonsense with Belinda. I don't mind it from other people. Get it?" You looked at your watch. "Aren't you running late?"

"Fuck that! Are you kidding?"

"Idris, sit down."

"Are you cheating on me?"

"What if I am?"

"I'll leave you. You hear me? We are over!"

You shrugged again. "Okay."

"Okay?"

"Yes. Okay."

He started screaming, "You were a nobody when I married you, and this is how you repay me?"

"You've got it backward. You were the nobody, Idris, when we married. You could barely feed yourself. I gave you the money to pay for my bride price, remember?"

"Are you cheating on me?"

"Yes." You held his eyes as you answered. "Perhaps you should sit down as I suggested."

Dazed, he lowered himself into the chair. Idris was not a violent man but you reached down and held the can of mace in your bag just in case.

"Who is he?"

"Kel."

His eyes flashed. "The driver who resigned three months ago?"

"Yes."

His eyes narrowed as he connected the dots. "He told me he was starting a business—"

"Yes, a car-leasing company."

"You're funding it, aren't you?"

"Of course. Because he keeps proper records, makes returns, and is on course to make a profit by next year. After funding five—or is it six?—of your businesses, did you ever learn how to make a profit?"

"Slut! A married woman with a child is doing ashawo work. Aren't you ashamed?"

"No. Because I learned from you, Idris. First to do no dey pain."

"Ah! You're a wicked woman. Didn't I beg you enough?"

"Yes, you always begged. But you're a mad man."

"I am mad? You are cheating and I am mad? I will divorce you and take my child."

You started laughing. It sounded strange, like it belonged to someone else. When it stopped, you locked eyes with him. "You're a mad man because, even now you're whining like a little bitch about me, you're fucking your new secretary."

He jerked back in surprise.

"Oh, you thought I didn't know? Why would you think that after all the times I've caught you? I have been with you all of my adult life, Idris. You cheated, lied, and killed my self-esteem. Luckily, I found someone who's a million times more man than you. And yes, I intend to keep him. So here's what we'll do. We will file for divorce, cleanly without public washing of dirty linen. My lawyer says we should say that the marriage has broken down irretrievably. I will give you some things so you can comfortably maintain your lifestyle. I'll keep Grace, but I'll be generous with visitation rights."

You sighed.

"But if you fight this or even think of taking my child, I will take everything from you. Your cars, your office, your lifestyle, everything that I funded while you went around launching one useless start-up after the other. Let me see how the Lagos girls you pose for will rate you after you drop from a G-Wagon to Uber."

He slouched in the chair, stunned.

You stretched a hand. "Give me my phone, Idris."

It took a long moment before he handed it to you. As you took it, you smiled and said, "It took you five days to find the text message even when I unlocked the phone, opened the message, and left it by your side of the bed. Disappointing, really."

You walked out.

CATFISH

Donald "Don" Okoro

As the driver turns into Ikeja GRA, I feel my dick rise in excitement. I'm not going home to Magodo, even when I know that my boys will be waiting for me. I have other ideas, thanks to Dooshima, my Instagram baddie.

I got back into Lagos barely an hour ago, having cut short my six-month music tour. When I started this music thing, people laughed at me. They made fun of everything about me, from my sound to my looks. It never bothered me. After three years of hard work, of hustling gigs wherever I could find them, of countless studio sessions, I am now an artist on the come up. I have worked with A-list musicians and producers. Finally, I am getting the recognition I deserve. The thing with Nigerians is that once you have their attention, you better show them you deserve it, otherwise you can become a forgotten has-been artist at any time. That is why my manager booked this tour.

But today is not about me. Today is for Dooshima. We have been chatting for a few weeks. I met her on Instagram, stumbled across her picture—she was stunning, perhaps the most beautiful girl I had ever seen. But sliding into a babe's DM on Instagram in this age of #MeToo and #MenAreScum, especially for an artist on the come up who had something to lose, took some courage and a dose of recklessness. But at the same time, I didn't want anyone to air me out on Instablog, abeg. My career did not yet have shock absorbers for scandals.

The babe was fiiinne sha. So, after two days of staring at her pictures, I gave in to temptation. I tested the waters by replying to one of her stories with an emoji. She responded. We chatted for a bit, moved to WhatsApp, and then one night after performing in Benin, we were chatting when shit went right.

Hey.

Heyyy, how was your show?

Mad o. The crowd knew all my songs. It was mad.

Yay! I am happy for you.

Thanks, Mami. I'm tired. Oh ☹

What's wrong?

I'm horny.

For real? Okay, Brb.

I am not even going to lie, I suddenly forgot that I was tired. I excused myself from the after-party, ran back to my hotel room, and texted:

Can I call?

No.

Video?

Not a good time.

Shit, Mami. Okay let's chat. Wish I could see you.

Really? What would you do?

Omo! I knew this was it. We had flirted a few times but *this* was different. This was heading somewhere good. I ran to the bathroom, grabbed my lotion. I was already hard; I had not had sex in two months. My mum, the overbearing prayer warrior, had made me promise to abstain from sex while on tour. "Don't let those women take away your star, Donald, avoid sex," she'd said.

It's been me and her since my father died after a brief illness five years ago. I really try to be a good son sha. So, before that night, before Dooshima, my Instagram baddie, came into the mix, it had been just my lotion and I. But this didn't have to end as a random on-tour virtual fuck. If I played my cards right, I just might be able to fuck her for real when I got back to Lagos. But for the moment, I sha had to hustle my orgasm.

Mami, I want to taste you. I want some of that juice.
It's been a while I got some.

                    Oh yeah? How long has it been?

Too long.

                    Tell me how you would make me wet.

First, I will go down between your legs.

                    What do you think my pussy would look like?

Fat. Warm. Wet.

                    What would you do when you see it?

I'll tease your clit with my tongue. I'll spell your name with the tip.

                    Oh wow, and then?

Then I'll slide my tongue in and out of your pussy.

Oh my god.

Would that feel good?

You're killing me, Don. My knees are shaking.

I'm soaking wet.

I want to suck those nipples that look like berries.

I want to ride you, I want that big dick in my mouth,

I want to choke on it.

I came all over the sheets. The girl was nasty. I liked that. From that night, we constantly sexted, and whenever she could, she did a striptease. Touching myself had become a sweet pain. I needed her; my whole body was on fire and I could not wait to get to Lagos to see her. That is why I called my manager last night to tell him I needed a break.

"Oga, we are in Ikeja," the driver says, interrupting my thoughts.

Quickly, I send her a message.

Hey Mami.

Hey Papi.

What are you up to?

                              Nothing. Just home with my flatie.

For real? Send a picture.

My phone buzzes. In the picture, she is lying in bed, wearing denim bum shorts and a flimsy cream-colored top, looking very sexy. Her flatmate is in the picture too, fast asleep beside her.

You are so hot.

                              Thank you, Papi.

I'm in Lagos and I'm on your street.

                              Whattttt!!! Stop it.

I'm serious.

She calls me immediately. "Are you for real?"

"Yup. I wanted to surprise you."

"I am so excited. See you soon, Papi."

Once I get off the phone, I tap the back of my jeans, satisfied with the reassuring bounce of my pack of condoms—I have six in total.

Today, we die here!

Dooshima

I'm screwed. Why now? Why can't a Lagos man ever surprise you with money or a car? They just show up and say "Surprise!" Oga, what manner of surprise is this? How can Don just show up in Lagos, on my street, without informing me? I shake Edikan, my flatmate, out of her sleep.

"What is it now?"

"You have put me in trouble o. Don is here."

Her eyes snap awake and she sits up immediately. "DON DON? Are you serious?"

"My friend, will you calm down? I'm freaking out here."

"Why?"

"Because he may want to knack."

"And?"

"And I'm not ready."

"My dear, do what you have to do to get ready because your vagina is going to sing tonight," Edikan teases. She starts playing one of Don's songs on her phone.

I can feel my insides turning to jelly. How do I hold him off? I had thought we would not see for another three months because of his tour so I figured I still had time to learn from Edikan how to be a bad girl on and off Instagram.

The dating scene in Lagos is full of frogs and virtually no princes. I learned that the hard way. And you know something else? Good girls don't exist in this social media age. They're a dying breed. Nobody wants the kind of wife material the mummies were designing years ago. If you're not a baddie you won't get a boyfriend, not to talk of a husband. Well, maybe in the hinterlands, certainly not in Lagos. And certainly not if you want prime male material like Don. Handsome, no scandals, and talented. Not to mention wealthy.

I have been a Unilag undergraduate for six years thanks to spillovers, lecherous lecturers, and strikes. If not for my parents and older brother sending me an allowance and my small side hustle doing marketing for a mobile accessory company, I wouldn't even be able to afford the rent I split with Edikan. Times are hard and they are even harder for so-called good girls. I'm tired of struggling, tired of sacrificing, and I am ready to do what it takes to secure a stress-free future for myself.

I had just revamped my image on Instagram and taken down all my old photos after my last relationship when Don sent me the first DM. Things ended badly between my ex and me. Let's just say I was a naïve good girl then. Cooking, cleaning, and encouraging Soji, meanwhile he was getting his knacks on with every girl north of the Lekki Toll Gate. He said I was boring. Imagine? I went to Edikan for help and she had been teaching me how to spice up my bland self. I was just getting used to being sexy in pictures when Don found me and we started chatting.

Edikan was the one who told me what to post, how to

pose and tease men. I had been taking pictures and posting for two months but all the men coming on to me had been disappointing. I can never understand how you will think you can shoot your shot with an Instagram baddie when your page has two pictures with you posing with the peace sign. The ones that had money or looked like they did were either too yellow for my taste or clearly married. I wanted a guy I could post and tag #CoupleGoals, not someone who will land me on Instablog. Those people and their followers are brutal.

Edikan encouraged me to keep looking and posting. Finally, the gods of Instagram answered my prayers with Don. I couldn't believe it. I knew it was not a fake account because it was verified.

So, me Dooshima, can catch a whole celebrity? I was so happy. I showed Edikan and she started telling me what to say. We chatted for a couple of weeks, then one night, Edikan changed the mood of our chats.

"Babe, you know this guy is a celeb, you need to keep him interested."

"He is interested na. We talk every day."

"With all those big-ass dancers he goes around with, you better start sexting him."

"Haba. No na. That seems a bit desperate."

"Okay, don't say I didn't warn you."

I dismissed Edikan's advice, but that night, Don didn't

chat with me so I started to think she was right. I needed to keep him interested. I went to her the next night, and that's how Don and I started sexting.

I had to learn to make fake sex noises, I even learnt to talk with a drawl. I started sending him videos of me in lingerie that Edikan lent me. We chatted more and I knew I had found my celebrity boyfriend. His tour was supposed to be for six months so I figured by then he would have fallen in love with me. Who knew he would show up unannounced today? The memory of Soji telling me that I am boring still lingers in my mind. I can't have that happen to me again.

"Today is the day my flatmate sleeps with a celebrity!" Edikan sang all over the house. I need to think fast.

I have to delay this for some time. I am a smart girl, after all.

Gosh, I hate this kind of surprise.

Don

Hmm. Her boobs are smaller in real life. I watch them as she runs toward me. I feel a twinge of disappointment as I had hoped to motorboat them later. I learned about motorboating on tour. After one performance in Abuja, our crew brought in some hot strippers.

"Don, pick one of the girls, let's go and have fun."

"I am good, Baba, I dey try abstain from knacking."

"No . . . no knacks, we go just play with them."

So I walked up to one of the girls who looked like she was comfortable being naked and he picked a petite, light-skin one. We went into the room and he showed me motorboating along with other tricks. Mehn, that night was wild.

I hope this night with Dooshima is wilder as I plan to release tension and relax. She is saying a lot but all I can think about is how fine she is. Her lips are so sexy, I am just nodding and agreeing to whatever words are coming out of that fuckable mouth. I have a face cap on so people don't recognize me as she leads me into her apartment.

Her place reminds me of my university days. When I get inside, I marvel at how she is able to cram so much in a space so little, every piece looks like it was customized to fit. There is a living room and two rooms. She shares a bathroom and kitchen with her roommate. I can't help but smile. Girls and their management skills. She is so flighty; her breasts are slapping each other due to her restlessness. I can't help but compare them to that beat in the studio that always moves too fast for my Afrocentric style. I hope she is not like this in bed. My dick is rising again as I think about us fucking.

She is saying a lot at once and nothing but I pretend to be listening. I just remembered I didn't get her anything. Nigerian girls take that kind of behavior seriously so I make a mental note to send her money before I leave the next day. If all goes well, I will invite her to Magodo.

Let's just see how this night goes first.

"Don, let's go clubbing," she says very close to my ear.

"Clubbing? Oh, really, babe? I want us to spend time together. If you don't want us to stay here, we can go to a hotel."

"No, we will come back here. I just want us to hang out for a while. Do you mind if my flatmate comes along?"

Of course I mind. Why do girls always bring their friends on dates? I smile to hide my irritation.

"I don't mind. The more the merrier. There is even this club that has been inviting me for months. Let me call my manager, I'm sure he can work out something."

"Thank you!" she says and runs into another room. I guess she is shy. Well, the shy ones are usually the freaks.

I can't wait to get freaky with her.

Dooshima

He has agreed to go clubbing with me and Edikan. I plan to keep the champagne flowing, I know he can afford it. I hope he gets drunk and has a limp dick. Although he seems to be cheap. The way he suggested that we go to a club where he had been asked to visit connotes stinginess. God, please, I can't deal with another cheap man. He must drop something before he leaves tomorrow.

My plan is simple. Get him drunk, as in puking-on-the-floor kind of drunk. Come back home, give him a hand job at best, I have mastered the art of hand jobs, then strip him naked so the next morning he thinks we had sex. Then when he wakes up, I will lie that I am traveling, then I will keep him keen with sex talk. Once I'm an expert, I will set a date and blow his mind.

For now, I will keep him engaged with the tricks Edikan has taught me.

Don

"EDIKAN! You can pronounce it like EH-DEE-CAN," the flatmate screamed over the music into my ears. I have no choice but to talk to her, she is seated between us at the club. I am not sure what is happening. I thought by now, Dooshima and I would have our tongues in each other's mouth but she has just been shoving drinks down my throat.

I don't want to be too drunk when we get back to her house. I am three glasses of Hennessy away from talking nonsense.

I wish Dooshima would stop dodging me. We arrived at the club two hours ago. Thankfully, the crowd wasn't too aggressive, I took a few pictures, signed some cleavages, and we were taken into the VVIP section.

The club is not too far from her house, it is perfect. I've set the flatmate up with one of the guys in the club so I am now closer to Dooshima. Gosh, she has sexy lips. I just want to suck on them. I am so horny.

"I am happy we have met!" I try to whisper in her ear, but

the speaker close to our sitting area keeps cutting our conversation short.

"Me too!"

"We can leave whenever you are ready." I run my fingers down her arm to buttress my point.

"It's okay. Let's stay. Edikan is having so much fun."

For fuck's sake! What do I care about the level of fun her flatmate is having? Does she not know how critical this situation is?

Dooshima

Did I leave the tap in my bathroom running? I hope not, I keep making this mistake. I don't want to come home to a flooded room—Oh my goodness! Why is this man determined to gum body with me this night? He keeps touching my knees and my butt. I see him looking at my boobs. Maybe I will let him suck them so he can at least be happy.

He is not drinking enough. I have tried to push him to drink. He just takes sips. I tried to put Edikan as a buffer but now he is sitting close to me. I am so glad the speaker is near our side of the club.

Edikan is talking to one of the guys that came to sit with us. I wish she would look my way so I can ask her to keep Don away from me. He wants us to leave but I don't think he is drunk enough.

"Dooshima, you are so pretty," he says.

"Thank you."

"I—"

The boom of the speaker drowns out his words.

"I'm sorry, I can't hear you. Please, excuse me. I need to go to the ladies." I pull Edikan away from her companion and drag her with me to the convenience. "Babes, Don is not drinking enough. What do I do?"

"Pour the Hennessy in your mouth, let him drink from there."

"So, I should feed a grown man from my mouth?"

"You make it sound so crude."

"Not just crude. Disgusting."

"Babe. You need to loosen up and drink some more sef because tonight you go do work o," she says, eyeing my waist.

"Will you stop?"

When we go back into the club, he's waiting at the entrance ready to leave.

"Hey! Dooshima! Over here!" Don calls out.

My heart drops.

Shit!

Dooshima

We are on our way to my apartment. Edikan is in front with the Uber driver, Don and I are at the back. He is about to kiss me.

"Babe, stop, we are not alone."

"So? She is not paying us any attention. I have been wanting to kiss you since I got here. Kiss me, baby."

"Just wait. We are almost home." I kiss his cheek and rest my head on his shoulders.

How do I get out of this night?

Don

Why is this girl not using her tongue? We got home a few minutes ago. I was so excited to enter her room. Now the flatmate is out of our way. I grabbed her and kissed her. Maybe I am going too fast but you can't blame me. I have been waiting.

I want to rip off her flimsy dress, but I don't want to seem too eager. So I settle for fondling her breasts, squeezing her butt, and kissing her.

Why is she playing hide-and-seek with her tongue? Is this a new sexual game?

Hold up. Did she just bite me?

Dooshima

This man is filthy. Haba. Why can't he take a shower and brush his teeth before kissing me? He reeks of cigarettes, Hennessy, and that perfume every man in Lagos owns, Sauvage. I smell it everywhere. He needs to shower; I need to shower. I don't want to taste cigarettes and alcohol. Ohhhh.

He's trying to stick his tongue down my throat. Jesus. Maybe if I close my teeth, he will get the message.

Oh shit. Did I just bite him?

Don

Okay, let me try to help her relax, maybe she is not into kissing, maybe she just wants my big dick. I don't know why she won't relax. Can she just stay still?

Omo. Why is she so dry? Let me try to suck her nipples and bite her ears. Kai. She is still dry o. I guess we are going to have to use lube. I reach out to grab my bag, but next thing I find myself almost on the floor. Did she just push me off her and move to the other side of the bed?

I don't understand, why is this girl acting like a weirdo? Is she serious? Am I supposed to be turned on by this? Na blue balls go kill me this night sha.

Let me try talking to her.

"Hey, are you okay?"

"I am."

"Do you need a drink? I have some cognac in my box. We can drink to relax."

"No. I am fine."

Sigh. Something is not right. This cannot be the girl I met on Instagram. What happened to the baddie who looked like she could swallow ten inches? Why is she staring at my dick like it is a strange object? I pull her into my arms and I try kissing her again. She's still not responsive. My dick no longer cares. I pull on a condom and try to shove it into her.

She is just lying there like a log of wood.

What kind of scam is this one? I'm so revved up that it doesn't take up to ten strokes to blow my load. I roll off her and turn to face her.

Can you believe that this stupid girl is sleeping? She is even snoring after doing absolutely nothing. I pick up my phone to hit up my ex, Kemi. She will stress me but at least the fuck will be awesome. I need a quick fix to rid my mind of the sad action that happened tonight. I check her status. Damn, she is at a concert.

I just had the worst sex in my adult life but I have already forgiven and forgotten her. If the roles were reversed, this babe will be nagging me now, before morning all her friends would have found out that I'm a lame fuck. But I'll just take this L. Sometimes, you shoot and miss.

I make one final attempt to text Kemi. She leaves me on read.

I am thirsty. Let me check if this babe has water. I think I saw a dispenser in the living room.

Edikan

He's finally come out. I have been waiting.

The moment we got back from the club, I changed my sheets, took a hot bath, and rubbed the scented oils I got from my Dubai connect. Then I put on my sexiest bra and panties, sat outside, and waited. I knew he would come out.

Tonight, he is going to be fucked like he has never been fucked before.

All through the evening, he had his eyes on Dooshima. I wanted to slap him and say, "Na me be the real babe. Yes, I am not as fine as her but I can ride you till your eyes roll back."

I have always known I am not a looker, but I refuse to date down. I have done that before, waste of time, now I need to level up. I know I can't attract the kind of guy I want with my looks, so enter Dooshima! We met at a party, and I targeted her not just because of her looks, but because she is a novice. I could tell from the way she danced; they say hips don't lie, well, hers tell a story. She doesn't know jack. I befriended her easily and got to work on my plan. Let me tell you something about this world we live in—you have to hustle your happy ending. Society says girls like me deserve dust and girls like Dooshima, the stars. Yeah, she's pretty, all right. But guess what, everything I have south of my average face is worth ten Dooshimas. Take it from me.

Once I made her my friend, I gave her a makeover. It wasn't hard for me to get some clothes for her since I run an online shop on Insta. She was just an ordinary fine but clueless babe with no fashion sense or taste. Two months makeover off and online and she became a baddie. The babe thought I was doing it out of the kindness of my heart, or that I was doing big sister with her. Lol.

No. This is Lagos. I was doing it for me. I knew whoever she caught was going to be mine. When she caught Don, I knew my prayers had been answered. I had hoped for an oil magnate or a politician, but I will take what I can get. Don has a bright future ahead of him. I can already see him being my baby daddy.

The moment he steps out and his gaze settles on me, I see his eyes light up as he takes in my voluptuous figure in my lingerie. I stretch my out hand to him.

"Come," I command with a whisper.

He steps forward with his mouth hanging open like one in a trance and takes my hand. I lead him into my room. I shut the door and push him till his back is against the door, and then I put my hand into his briefs and begin to massage his already hard dick, gently, while rubbing the top of his head. I bend his head to my lips, kiss him deeply using my tongue to search out his secrets. I draw back to trace his neck with my tongue. I feel him shiver as I trace his ear with my tongue and then I bite the left lobe lightly. I walk him to the bed, push him on it, and then I tie his hands over his head and spread his feet apart. I take off his briefs and his dick springs out. I smile, kneel between his legs, take him into my mouth, and then I begin to suck him. I play with his balls as I suck harder. He is trembling and I can feel he wants to cum so I pull my lips away. As I crawl up, nestling his warm dick between my thick thighs, I put my finger in his mouth, then rub the finger on my nipples.

"I need water . . . please," he gasps.

I stretch over him and get a sachet of water from the side of my bed. I feed it to him while kissing him in between. He drinks from both pools greedily.

Putting the water sachet on the drawer, I bring out a condom and roll it onto his dick. Pushing my thong aside, I straddle him. I start riding him, making slow, drawn-out up-and-down motions. The look on his face is priceless—I own him. I lean forward and put a nipple in his mouth while riding. I tease him, making it hard for him to suck the nipple properly as it keeps bouncing out of his reach. I increase the motion, pausing in between thrusts to milk him with my pussy, squeezing and contorting. The veins on his forehead look like they are going to pop out, so I cover his mouth with mine. I repeat this move three times, then I ride him hard. He comes fast, heaving and gasping.

I am not done.

I loosen his hands.

"Do you promise to be quiet?"

He nods like a little boy eager for a present from his mummy. I bring a bottle of coconut oil, take two of his fingers, put some oil on them, and bring him against my clit.

"Fuck me hard."

He starts to finger me, the oil creating a warm fuzzy feeling in me. Moments later, I take his fingers out, lick them, wet my fingers, and begin to pleasure myself while he watches. I finger myself until I come in a wave that leaves me breathless. As I climax, I can see his dick grow hard so I lean over, rub some oil on it, and then I bend over so he can push into me. He kneels behind me, uses one hand to rip my thong apart, and begins to thrust. I hold on tight to my bed stand but it keeps making noises. Even me, I cannot control myself again, so I moan out loud and call his name. I don't care. His dick keeps getting bigger inside me. He starts to slap my ass as he increases the pace of his thrusts.

I love it!

Somewhere inside this sweetness I hear Dooshima scream, "What the fuck is going on here?"

I look up. She is standing by the door looking like a bruised angel in her thigh-length lace nightie.

Don stops for a moment. Dooshima flees. I know he wants to go after her but I push my wet pussy higher so he can go deeper.

He groans.

"Don't stop," I command.

He starts ramming into me again. We come seconds after and I just hold his hands against my breasts, breathing heavily as he sinks on top of me.

"What is your name again?" he asks after an eternity.

I smile.

Don

I didn't fuck Edikan, she fucked me, I swear. I wanted to run after Dooshima but I had to finish. No man in his right mind leaves a pussy that tight. That was the best sex of my life. Who knew the night was going to turn out this way? I know Dooshima is never going to forgive me, so what is the point of begging? Kemi that I broke her heart two years ago is still not talking to me.

I look over at Edikan lying next to me. This girl has mind o but I like it. We need to do this again. This time in Magodo.

I lean in to kiss Edikan.

In this life you have to hustle for your orgasms. This is me hustling for as many orgasms as I can collect.

Tonight, I die here.

SIDELINED

When you met him, you were living a small life tainted by big dreams. In a corner of the single room that Ini, your best friend from childhood, generously let you move into when you first arrived from Enugu, stood evidence of another failed hustle that had seemed so promising. Those faux Italian, snakeskin leather bags were supposed to sell like hotcakes. They came in trendy colors, fuchsia surprise, plum sunrise. You had imagined building a small enterprise on the back of sales from Instagram and word of mouth, imagined micro-influencers giving you free marketing as they paraded them on their pages as part of their "outfit of the day" and tagging your business account. You even imagined typing your name in the account header with "CEO" next to it, and the rush of accomplishment you would feel that you came to Lagos and hacked it so quickly.

Yet there the bags were, mostly unsold, the trend for

bright "ashawo" colors having become passé, and with only a third of the consignment you paid for with your hard-earned savings sold.

Ambition is lifeblood for girls like you, second nature. A gateway to a successful life that has very specific dimensions: the respect and envy of others, the support and validation of friends and family, and the love and devotion of the man of your choosing. After the business hustle crashed, sure you were sad, but you changed tack and started applying in earnest for any and every job you could find, whether you were truly qualified or not. Until your life took a sudden, unexpected turn.

When your phone rang that day three years ago, you were in your room plaiting Ini's daughter's full, bushy mane, taming it into neat rows for school the next day. You and Ini had gone through everything together; you were the first person she told the day she met her husband, you talked her through their every fight and hiccup, and when she eventually married and gave birth to your goddaughter Treasure, you were right there to wipe the white gunk off the newborn's skin.

It was only natural that she would be there for you when you came to Lagos, with your dreams in one hand, your luggage in another, and no home to call your own.

"I am not your mother o, I will beat you," you threatened Treasure as she struggled against your hands trying to make a single twist from her 4C hair; even though you knew you would never touch her, you loved the coconut head too much to hurt her and the little twat knew it.

"If you beat me, I will not play with you again," she countered.

You had been thinking about how much you enjoyed playing hide-and-seek with Treasure even though she wasn't particularly good at hiding, when the strange number called your phone.

"Hello?" You answered on the first ring.

"Hello, is this a Miss Genevieve Ndala?"

"Yes, this is Genny." You had assumed that the company you'd interviewed for in Maryland was calling, it being a weekend notwithstanding.

"Ah, okay. My name is Odili. I am sorry to call like this but I had no choice. I don't want us to start on a lie so let me just say it. I saw you pick up a delivery from the front of your gate. I paid the delivery man for your number. Please don't be angry."

At the time of Odili's phone call, you were twenty-nine years old. That terrible age, that cusp before the decade of womanhood where you had to have something of value to show society. But you had nothing. Your education, skills, and beauty, none of that had yielded any dividends. You had discovered that Lagos was full of women like you, hustling, not-so-bad women. However, the threat of failure had sharpened your senses to the scent of opportunity, of a break, a chance. Maybe that's why you didn't cut the call on the weirdo calling you on a Sunday morning with no clear objective.

You told yourself instead that it was his honesty or the uncertainty in his voice that made you say, "I am not angry, Mr. Odili. How can I help you?"

"Please, call me Oddy."

"Okay, Oddy."

He came in like a tsunami and took over your life. A mere three weeks after that Sunday call and he had secured you your first job. Another couple of weeks later, your back was pressed against the passenger window of the luxurious interior of his car in your first kiss as a couple. You went from "I" to "we" in a matter of months. Oddy wasn't particularly handsome but the angles of his face were bold, his nose sturdy. A keenly intelligent man with no air of civilization that he didn't bother to hide. But he was gentle with you. Everything that concerned you mattered to him. He taught you about sex and pleasure, something you had not explored in your past relationships.

One night in a suite at Eko Hotels, you were sitting on the bed in a fluffy white bathrobe when he sat across from you, a towel loosely tied around his waist, and said, "I want to watch you touch yourself."

"I can't do that, Oddy."

"It is your body, of course you can."

"It's weird."

"Watch me, then."

He loosened the towel to reveal his penis. He gently ran his hand along its length. Your body filled with molten heat as it became engorged, the pleasure of his hand rubbing slick oil over his thickening, veined penis contorting his face until he released the tension into his palm. He cleaned himself with a wipe.

Then he took your finger, dipped it into his mouth; the heat of the walls of his mouth as he moistened your finger made you feel warm and heady. Parting your bathrobe, he took the finger and slipped it into your panties.

"Do it."

You put the finger into yourself and started moving it in and out. You watched him watch you, and before everything became blurry you saw that he was hard again, he started stroking himself and you both finished together.

You had sex everywhere. Your body became like a finely tuned instrument to his desires. Just one look across the room would have your knees trembling and the walls of your pussy throbbing. He once pulled the car over in a secluded corner of V.I. to spread your thighs open and eat you out. You've been bent over, the tips of your manicured fingers barely touching the carpet as he thrust into you, the view of

Dubai from the top of your suite blurring as you came together.

What was it about being with Oddy that was so intoxicating? It wasn't just the sex, incredible as it was. You had never met anyone quite like him. All the other men you had dated were dreamers like you, plotters of an uncertain future. Oddy appeared in your life fully formed. There was a power he possessed that you were deeply drawn to. But when you talked to Isi about him you couldn't always read the expression on her face. On the day you quit your job six months into it because he had said, a few days before a business trip to Dubai, "Babe, you need to come with me before these girls tempt me, just leave your work and follow me," her objection was swift and damning.

"Genny. Do you think this is wise? Is this relationship not moving too fast?"

The walls of Ini's guest room that had seemed safe now felt restrictive. The fact that you had to talk about Oddy in late-night whispers after Treasure had gone to bed and never mention him around her husband because of what he might think made it even more stifling. You smiled sweetly at your friend and said, "Maybe it's fast because I have been waiting so long for something good to happen to me."

What you were really thinking of was how Ini had told you that Lagos would be hard before it was easy. That the best start you could get was living with her in Lekki, and now that luck had finally favored you, she seemed more concerned than happy.

In no time, you became Oddy's disciple, you followed him everywhere and the rewards were the designer shoes and bags, the investments, and even the house you would eventually have to sell because too many memories of him lingered there.

"We can't keep sleeping in hotels when I am in Lagos. Get a house. We can stay there together," he said a year after you had quit your job. "Coming home to you is all I need, Genevieve."

You should have asked more questions, but in those early, enchanting days of being around Oddy you were too busy being swept away by the experience to examine it. You knew he traveled a lot for business, but even roaming birds come home to a nest. Why did you not ask where he stayed when you were apart?

A month later, you found a place in Lekki Phase 1. You nearly fainted when the house agent gave you the costing but Oddy paid immediately.

"Baby, this house is expensive."

"Baby, it is not."

"We can find somewhere cheaper, maybe smaller? We don't need three bedrooms."

"Think about traffic, my love. Also, what happens when I want a quickie? I should drive through all that traffic?"

"All you think about is sex," you had joked with him.

"Incorrect. I also think about money."

You moved in together. You could not travel with him all the time, so the house was a wise choice. He wouldn't let you work, so you had to find ways to keep busy. You registered at a fitness center, took up cooking classes, made new friends. Funny how all the things you did to preoccupy yourself when he traveled became the things you fell back on when he left. Treasure and Ini came often, taking up the guest room and making the house less lonely.

"So, when is Oddy going to do right by you? It has been a year and half. Is he waiting for God to show him a sign?" Ini asked with her usual expression, her lips pinched into a hyphen and her big brown eyes probing into you. She always had the gift of cutting through the bullshit. A gift you hated and loved.

You wanted to tell her that it already felt like you were married. When he was home you cooked all his best dishes and ate together. He even brought some business friends over to watch Chelsea lose to Man U over beers and asun as you hovered between the kitchen and the living room. Asking for more seemed greedy, even to someone as ambitious as yourself.

Instead, you said, "Ini, abeg, this is 2019. Don't start.

We are in love, happy, and he takes care of me. That is enough."

"Please shut up, Genevieve, you are not getting younger, he needs to marry you."

"I don't have the energy to argue with you. Treasure, come and see the car Uncle Oddy bought for you."

"Mummy said I should not collect any gift from Uncle Oddy until he marries you. Has he married you, Aunty?"

You distracted Treasure by switching the channel over to Nick Jr., and with fire in your eyes, you had turned on Ini. Speaking in a strangled whisper, you said, "Why will you bring Treasure into this, please?"

"He should buy you a ring and stop buying toy cars for other people's children. He needs to marry you and give you babies, so that Treasure can deal with them," Ini stubbornly whispered back.

Oddy never used protection when you had sex but his pull-out game was masterful. On the few occasions when he wasn't certain, you willingly took the Postinor tablet he left for you.

"You are a witch, this girl," you said, throwing a cushion at her as she hissed.

After they left, Ini's words stayed with you. You remembered an evening six months ago, when the paint in the house was barely dry and the furniture newly assembled. He had come home from a seminar; he sat in the living room and ate white soup with eba. He always liked for you to sit next to him so you could eat and talk. A habit you never knew was possible until you relocated to Lagos.

Back at home, you ate in silence punctuated by bone cracking, gulping, and the sound of your father clearing his throat. Oddy didn't particularly care for table manners.

You had always found it amusing.

That evening, he looked across to you as you ate together and said, "Genevieve, will you date me?" He devoured a piece of stockfish, at the same time trying to catch the drops of white soup dripping down his pinkie. You were surprised. After a year, after everything you had seen and done together, you wondered where this was coming from. When you didn't respond immediately, he looked at you again and said, "What?"

"It's just . . . what were we doing before now?" you responded as you leaned over to wipe the corner of his mouth.

"I just want to make it official," he said and continued to eat. When you said yes, he never again called you Genny. You were his baby, and he refused to call you anything else.

"You are my baby. I love you and I will continue to love you."

At the time, you concluded: that was enough.

Your father decided he wanted to come to Lagos to see for himself how well you were doing. He whistled when he set his bags down and looked around your apartment. He looked at you with his slightly rheumy eyes and you thought there might have been a glint of respect in there.

Did it bother you that he thought the house and car were part of a package deal from your high-flying marketing job in Victoria Island? No. Neither did the fact that you felt relieved that Oddy was away on a business trip when your father had called to say he was at the airport. All relationships proceed in stages; you and Oddy were not yet at the point where meeting fathers was necessary. It didn't make things between you less real. Your father looked around the living room and whistled again, his hands on his waist.

"This place is ideal for children to run about," he said, turning around to look at you. "Don't get too comfortable being alone, enjoying yourself, that you will forget what matters."

My father is old-fashioned, you thought. A career civil servant who upon retirement spends his time attending one community gathering or the other, doling advice to people. Your mother had to spend the better part of a year using all the tricks in her arsenal persuading him to allow you to leave home for Lagos. You smiled and gently directed him to the spare room.

True to type he spent a mere two days with you and hastened back to Enugu. That weekend, when Oddy showed up to whisk you off to Accra, you told yourself as you packed your suitcase that you were lucky, possibly the luckiest girl in Lagos.

How much do you need to know about a person to be in love with them? You had so many conversations as you ate together, sat in the departure lounges of airports, or wrapped your sticky bodies around each other in one hotel room or the other. Oddy had a way with words; he loved to talk and you loved to listen. Some of his anecdotes you knew by heart because you had heard them so often.

"Do you know I was a bricklayer for four years? In those years, I watched the rich men that we built houses for, I studied them, and baby, I knew at that point, I wanted to be one of them."

He shared his money and experiences with you freely. Sometimes you wondered if he did not feel his tongue was a bit too loose around you. Whatever defenses you might have put around your heart crumbled over time because he gave you no reason to doubt his sincerity and honesty. When you asked him about his birthday, he said, "February 29." You did some quick thinking and scowled in disbelief. "I'm serious," he said with that bubbling laugh that spilled over to his shoulders and made his eyes come alive.

"You see me? I'm only twelve years old now as I'm talking to you," he said, still laughing.

Because you were with him for only three years, and never saw a leap year together, you never celebrated his birthday, never bought him a birthday cake. On yours, he would send piles of gifts and transfer more money than you needed to throw a party for a community, but he never showed up. He also didn't like his picture taken, something about a phobia. No matter where you were in the world, in front of the Eiffel Tower in Paris, or in the kitchen as you both cleaned up after dinner, Oddy would never let you take a selfie together. And so your phone was filled with portraits he took of you, the only evidence of his existence being the smile in your eyes as you posed for him.

You escorted him on a trip to Abia State, where he had given a lecture about how to make money from forex. The small, air-conditioned hall had window drapes the color of the Nigerian flag. It was full to capacity. You watched people, some who didn't seem to know where their next meal would come from, tapping wildly into the dreams that Oddy sold them. They believed it so much that they manifested it. But Oddy's success formula wasn't for everyone. And those ones who didn't see their dreams come true put their anger into words and published negative reviews on Nairaland forums.

You had felt terrible reading the reviews.

Oddy didn't care about bad press. "Baby, publicity sells. You have to ignore the internet. They are mad people sitting behind keypads with nothing better to do. I know why I started forex trading. I want to help people. I know I am still doing that," Oddy would say. He transformed his own life learning how to trade, and he was convinced he could do the same for others.

In the end, the seminars were what revealed the truth of your situation to you.

That Saturday you were in the Ebeano Village Market shopping for ingredients to make some of Oddy's favorites. He had let you know on WhatsApp that morning that he was coming in from London in two days. At the payment point, you had run into one of the people who attended his seminar in March the previous year.

"Madam, good afternoon, you don't remember me?"

You cast him a perfunctory look—mid-thirties, bushy hair and beard, a hustler. "No, I'm sorry, please. Good afternoon."

"Oh, its fine." He beamed you a smile. "I attended your husband's seminar in March last year, see me now! I am a fully certified forex trader. I even just got married."

This stranger in two sentences reminded you of what was missing in your relationship. You had wanted to tell him that Oddy was not your husband but you stopped yourself.

You smiled and said, "Congratulations. I will tell Oddy I saw you. He is out of the country."

"Oh, please help me greet him, Ma."

The conversation lasted all of two minutes, but if you hadn't stopped to talk to him, you would have missed the couple walking into the main section of Ebeano just two steps ahead of you. The man had Oddy's characteristic swagger, he rolled his shoulders a little bit when he walked, with that majestic profile tipped toward the sky. The woman walking next to him was pregnant.

But he is in London. I must really miss him.

You had decided to put a call through to him on WhatsApp. You saw the man take his phone out of his pocket, and put it back.

It can't be. B-but I dropped him at the airport.

You were not quite aware that you were shuffling forward until you caught up with them. You didn't even realize it when your hand reached out and tapped the man's shoulder. He turned around. It was Oddy.

His face, eyes wide in surprise and quickly knotting in a frown and lips clenching into a thin line, was the last thing you saw before you were swallowed up by darkness. When you came to, the security guard and staff were waving pieces of paper frantically in your face. One of them had propped you into a sitting position. Oddy and the pregnant woman were hovering around you.

"Are you okay, young lady?" Oddy asked.

You searched for something to say but came up empty.

"Do you have anyone we can call? My husband and I were so worried when you fainted."

The man she called her husband looked like Oddy, sounded like Oddy—but you didn't know this man wearing Oddy's skin.

"I am fine."

You got into your car and drove home. You remained in the car, your trembling hands on the steering wheel, your body racked with silent sobs. Your phone vibrated on your lap. You picked it up—it was a message from Oddy: *You really didn't need to embarrass me like that. Why will you walk up to me in public? I am disappointed in you, Genevieve.*

All the signs were there. The wardrobe was full of your clothes, shoes, bags; his side held five shirts, two pairs of trousers, and one pair of shoes. Every time he "came home," he brought along his toiletries and other effects in a bag and left with them again. Your home together was always a transit stop. It was where you lived, but Oddy had always been a guest.

In the two days before he had showed up at the house,

you oscillated between disbelief and delusion. You told yourself that he must have been forced to marry the other woman for a reason you didn't yet know. It must have been hard on him being in love with two women and he didn't know how to handle it. You revisited those early days and wished you had agreed for him sooner, was that when someone else stepped in? Was she a business associate? She looked very old compared to you.

Because you spent all your time with him and had drifted apart from Ini, you courted this madness all by yourself. Your phone was full of people who would say, "I told you so." On this God's green earth, you were the last to know that you were being taken for a fool.

When the doorbell rang you stayed still for several seconds. The Oddy that you knew had never used it before. He called your name and you managed to peel yourself from the sofa that you had been stuck in and walk to the door. The moment he appeared in the door frame you knew that you had lost him.

He stepped into the room with the sobriety appropriate for a funeral. His hands in his pockets, the warm, rowdy persona you had so much loved tucked away from sight.

"I feel betrayed, Oddy," you said. He was dressed in a crisp striped shirt and tailored pants. You hadn't taken off your off-white T-shirt and Adidas joggers for two nights. You crossed your arms defensively against your chest, feeling vulnerable, knowing that the turmoil of the past forty-eight hours had been felt by you alone.

"Why? Wasn't I good to you? Did I ever hit you or scream? Did I not take care of you?"

"You were lying to me the whole time." You tried to keep the tears away from your voice but failed.

"I never lied because you never asked."

"You asked me to date you. Married men don't date other women!"

"Genny, come on. You knew the deal."

"Deal? What deal?"

"Look. I was happy with this arrangement until you pulled that stunt two days ago. In public of all places. What if my wife had figured things out? And even now you're showing no remorse."

My wife.

Those two words landed in your heart with the efficacy of gunshots fired by a skilled assassin.

"You are lucky I love you, Genny, because that nonsense could have ended this relationship," Oddy continued. He gave you a cold stare. There was a bitter curl to the corner of his mouth.

"How long?"

"What do you mean?"

"How long have you been married, Oddy? From the beginning?"

He bristled with impatience, moved to the window, parted the curtains, and looked outside.

Desperate for answers, you followed him. "Just tell me the truth, please."

"Genny, if we are to continue, I can't talk about my wife or kids with you. I like to keep my private life separate." He made a gesture with his hands cutting slices in the air.

As you stood face-to-face with him, everything fell into place and you started crying.

"Please stop. I have given you everything. I bought this house for you. What more do you want?"

You had cried until he left in irritation. You went into the bedroom, lay down, and slept for nearly twelve hours. When you woke up, you started bargaining with yourself. You were thirty-two, without a job or a plan. Shouldn't you just stay in Oddy's life even if it was on the sidelines? How long and cold was this shadow of a wife and kids? If you truly loved him, wouldn't you stay?

When you called him after a few days of reflection, you thought it was the network playing up when the robotic voice told you his number didn't exist. He had no Facebook page or Twitter handle that you knew of. Searching for his name on the internet brought up many images and name combinations, but none were the Oddy that you knew, none could tell you where he lived, or why he was no longer answering his phone.

So today, after three months of trying to reach him, questioning if the last three years had been a figment of your imagination, you will sit in the corner of your living room and cry because a married Lagos man broke your heart.

BEARD GANG

Your phone beeped at a few minutes past midnight. You glanced at it. The message read: *He says he is leaving me. HELP!!!!*

It was from Flora.

You sighed softly, irritated because you'd asked that no one send a message past 10 p.m. But it was just like Flora, the twit, to disobey simple instructions. It crossed your mind that she may have been distressed when she sent the message, but you remembered she was a drama queen, and it was more likely she sent it while lolling in her jacuzzi.

Still, she'd asked for help, from you, and from the group. And as the head of the group, you were obligated to help. You sighed again. Tapped your phone. Opened WhatsApp. Scrolled to the group titled Virtuous Wives Guild and typed: *Emergency meeting at 2 p.m.* Then you deleted Flora's message, and slipped your phone into the pocket of your silk house robe.

You walked down the imperial staircase to double-check if the foyer windows were locked. Since the time, fifteen years ago, when armed robbers walked into your former house at Anthony Village because the gateman was careless, you'd gotten understandably paranoid. Now, though you lived in Banana Island, arguably the most secure part of Lagos, and had a top private security firm guarding your mansion, you were still paranoid. So, every day, you double-checked all windows and doors, and didn't sleep until everyone was dozing. Check completed, you went back upstairs to your bedroom.

You settled into the white love seat near the foot of your king-size bed. As usual, you sat there for about an hour, watched Biodun, your husband, as he snored softly on the bed. And as usual, you prayed silently, first for the strength to get in bed with Biodun.

Your other nightly prayers were not for God's protection or help, but more about repeating your neurosis to him. Your life's journey—from crippling childhood poverty in Maroko till after you graduated from LASU; to the years of joblessness and semi-regular prostitution on the Allen Avenue and Opebi axis; to when you met Biodun in church (actually, you met him after church, when many of the congregation spilled out to Costain Bus Stop, and he assumed you were one of them, and you never corrected him); to the early years after your marriage when you lived hand-to-mouth in Anthony Village, where the robbers came; to when Biodun met Otunba, who became his benefactor and helped him become the billionaire he now was—was a remarkable one. But because you were a secret worrier, you never quite fully enjoyed the now because you were always scared that somehow you'd go back to being poor, or someone would expose your past.

Eventually, your prayers ended, you got in bed, but ensured you slept as far away as possible from your husband of twenty years.

You woke at 5 a.m. as usual and went through your routine—prayed (this time, for God to protect your children from the craziness in America and your husband from himself), did a thirty-minute Tabata workout at the home gym downstairs, showered, then woke Biodun at 6:30 a.m. to start his day.

As usual, you had breakfast together. Akara and ogi for him; half an avocado, a boiled egg, and black unsweetened coffee for you. As usual, breakfast was mostly quiet, interrupted by the soft beeps from Biodun's iPad Pro and the occasional small talk that came from the natural see-finish of two decades of marriage.

"I'm going out by one p.m.," you said. Biodun grunted his acknowledgement.

"I have a meeting at church. I should be back by three p.m." There was no need to explain, or lie, but you did both anyway. Force of habit.

"I'm going out later in the afternoon. Some young hot-shots who are trying to convince me to invest in their company have somehow blagged entry into the members' section of the Yacht Club, and want us to have a lunch meeting there. They think that will impress me?" He curled his lips. "Me, who has been a full boat-owning member for ten years?" He shook his head and went back to his screen.

As a dutiful wife, you tut-tutted your support for him and disapproval of the folly of the faceless young men. But you remembered years ago, when it was Biodun's big dream to be a member of the Yacht Club, and how servile he was to the members till Otunba nominated him for membership.

"How is Otunba?" you asked.

Biodun sighed wearily. "I saw him yesterday at his place. The old man is still frail and bedridden. Just wasting away slowly." He sighed again. "It's been three years, but he has never gotten over losing Lady Deborah, you know?"

"I know." You nodded. But you don't tell him you're surprised Otunba had lived this long after the death of Deborah, his wife. "I will go see him tomorrow and spend some time with him," you said. "I'll take him some chicken pepper soup and read to him. He likes that."

"That's nice. Please do."

"Will you be home by nine p.m.? I plan to call the boys by then. I was hoping we can talk to them together."

Since the Covid-19 pandemic prevented your thrice-yearly

travel to New York, you could only video call with your twin boys schooling at Columbia University. You missed them so much, you cried after the end of the last video call you had with them and Biodun. Puzzled, Biodun had asked, "They're grown men—why are you crying so much?" And you'd replied that your babies were still nineteen, nowhere near grown men, and you hadn't seen them in almost a year. Biodun had harrumphed because he'd never understand. Perhaps no one would understand that you cried because Kehinde, the picky eater, had lost some weight; and there was no way Taiwo, who was trying to grow dreadlocks, would have kept that ridiculous and unkempt hair if you had visited them in New York. But you didn't say you cried mostly because, after considering the darkness of your Allen Avenue days and the deep dissatisfaction of your marriage, sometimes you were overwhelmed with gratitude that you were the lucky mother to two beautifully perfect boys. They were the best and purest things in your life, a nod to God and his mysterious ways.

"I'll be back by nine to talk to them." He grunted and continued reading the news from his device. You guessed the small talk at breakfast was over.

You left for your meeting with the group around 1 p.m. You drove yourself in the 2014 Range Rover Sport, because it was the oldest and least ostentatious car in the house. On days like this, you'd have preferred to drive any of the pre-2010 black and battered Toyota Corollas ubiquitous in Lagos, but Biodun, the now-insufferable car snob, would never allow you drive anything so plebeian. You drove to the largely empty parking lot of the Church of the Nativity in Parkview. You waited.

The meeting was scheduled to be held in an Airbnb apartment in Lekki, somewhere behind Ebeano Supermarket. When Deborah started the group years ago with you as her first member, you could meet for lunch, or in each other's houses or cars, where you communicated in coded whispers. But as the group grew, meetings at homes or public places became riskier because no one could take the chance of a servant or waitstaff eavesdropping on the conversations.

You didn't wait for long. You watched a maroon Ford Edge drive into the church and park next to you. It was Gbonju, in her least ostentatious car. She was to give you a ride to and fro the meeting. You put on your big shades that covered half your face, stepped from your car, and slipped into Gbonju's. "Good afternoon, Aunty," she greeted you with a smile, as she slipped the SUV into gear and rolled out.

You always liked Gbonju, especially because she was punctual, respectful, and discreet for one so young. She was now thirty-two and had been married for eight years to Dipo, now an oil magnate, who you'd introduced to her when she was twenty-three. You'd chosen well with Gbonju. You'd chosen her for Dipo, who at the time was a rising mid-level executive in Biodun's oil company. The then-naïve girl had believed in their perfect whirlwind romance. To date, theirs was the biggest and most flamboyant wedding you'd attended in Nigeria. You know this because Biodun sponsored most of it. And as you'd sat at the wedding reception and watched Dipo and Gbonju feed each other cake, you caught Dipo's eye for a second, and you both remembered.

You'd both remembered that night, a year before. Somehow, Biodun had misheard the return date for one of your trips. You'd come home unannounced and walked to your bedroom. You'd found Biodun and Dipo, both naked on the bed. Biodun was spreadeagled, and Dipo, bent over Biodun with his hairy buttocks in the air, worked a slurpy blow job.

It was Deborah who had paid you a surprise visit the next morning. "I hear you've found your husband's secret," she'd said in her soft but firm voice. "Welcome to the club."

Your eyes had been puffy from crying all night, but you felt them pop. At that moment you knew—Biodun had been and probably was still to Otunba what Dipo was now to Biodun. Deborah, a woman of few words, had nodded her confirmation, and said, "Chin up, dear. These men, as much as we love them, are not worth our tears. Instead, allow me to show you the best way to thrive."

Her rationale was easy to understand. She had given the best years of her life to her marriage with Otunba before she discovered, eleven years and three children later, that he had used her to hide the fact he was gay. Instead of a divorce, which, in her opinion, would result in a chunk of Otunba's considerable wealth frittered away by his paramours, she opted to stay in the marriage. "I thought like a man and took a cold-blooded business decision. For myself and my children," she had explained. She couldn't stop Otunba, but she collared him somewhat. By a combination of the force of her personality and the logic in her arguments, she convinced Otunba to stop affairs with the undesirables (i.e., single, younger, poor men, some of whom were probably gay-for-pay and could resort to blackmail). The ideal choice for Otunba became men in bearded marriages, who had something to lose if their sexuality became public knowledge. It also helped if such men were industrious and smart—she understood they would make money for themselves and Otunba, rather than simply leech off him, and that way, everybody won. Biodun was such a man.

It was Deborah who, without telling you how, negotiated Biodun's apology to you. It came in the form of a transfer of twenty million naira to your account that evening, and an all-expense-paid holiday and shopping trip to New York for you and the boys. She also taught you how to stretch that apology till now without breaking it—by getting him to fund your international real estate and importation businesses. You were now worth twelve million dollars, and yes, you could have left Biodun a few years ago, and still be fine but, as Deborah always said, "Misery loves company, dear." She was also fond of asking rhetorically, "Why spend your money when you can spend his?"

So, yes, you just needed Biodun to finish paying the boys' fees at Columbia. Besides, over time, you'd grudgingly grown to tolerate and even like the idiot.

More important, because you learned well from Deborah, a year after finding out his secret, you'd gone to Biodun and said, "It's best for everyone if Dipo gets married soon. It'll protect both of you." And he'd nodded. And when you'd suggested Gbonju, who at the time was a bright girl trying to sell you insurance, it was sealed.

It was Deborah who took you under her wing, and quietly pointed out the closeted gay and bisexual men in Lagos high society, and the mostly clueless wives of those who were married. With Deborah, you attended the weddings of those who took wives later, where you gave lavish gifts and danced with some of them, while feeling sorry for all the wives. It was Deborah who came up with the idea to create a support group for some of these women. After all, she mused, your husbands had fucked most of their husbands.

But it was also Deborah who refused to tell you about the gluttonous cancer gobbling her insides till she had two months to live. She'd eventually told you, in a whisper, at her last meeting with the group. It was an unusual meeting because it was held publicly at a spa (Deborah's treat for all the women), and no business was discussed. After she'd told you, she'd smiled and wagged a weak finger at the sudden silent tears in your eyes. "Chin up, dear. I always gave as good as I got in this life."

Then she'd pointed to the other white-robed women lounging in beds with sliced cucumbers over their eyes and whispered, "You're the she-wolf now. Act like it."

It irritated you that you and Gbonju were the first to arrive for the meeting, and that Flora, at whose insistence the meeting was called, was not there yet.

"Aunty mi, so what's going on with Flora?" Gbonju asked.

You hissed. "Who knows? It's probably nothing, you know she's such an attention seeker, that one. Anyway, we'll find out when she gets here. Although you'd think she ought to be here early since it's her problem we are here to solve, no?"

Gbonju laughed. You liked how she never commented. Wise girl. You remembered a year into her marriage, she'd showed up at your office, pregnant and scowling, to whisper that she'd found out that Dipo was gay. She'd never given any details, but you suspected she'd found out about Dipo and Biodun, and that's why she'd come to you.

"Give birth to your child. Get your money up. Buy properties abroad in your name," you'd advised.

She'd listened. Now she had three villas, in the Algarve, Monaco, and Santorini, which she fully leased out to vacationers. You knew this because you bought and managed the villas for her through your international real estate agency.

Onome, the flamboyant one, came in. She was the quintessential Lagos Big Girl, gorgeous, fully designer-branded, and beloved of blogs and paparazzi. Her husband was a pastor, and so deeply closeted he might as well be buried in a coffin lost at sea. He had no scandals, had never been with a man as far as she was aware, but he'd admitted his sexuality to her. You didn't care much for Onome's ostentation, but you liked that she was carefree, didn't have wahala, and just loved the good life.

Fatima was next. The third wife of a northern senator, married off by her father to cement a formidable political alliance. She was easily one of the most beautiful women you'd seen. Yet she tiptoed around, unaware of the power she held in her face. She'd been painfully naïve and a virgin when she married the senator—a man thirty years older with two wives and seven children, and a ravenous sexual appetite. She found out her husband preferred men during their honeymoon in Dubai. She was surprised when he'd suggested they have a threesome, astounded when he brought in a man, and aghast when they went passionately at it leaving her as the unwelcome third wheel. Four months after her return to Nigeria, Onome brought her to you (they had been classmates and unlikely friends from their university days abroad). You'd accepted her. Now she had three children and her husband constantly bought her silence with expensive gifts.

"I'm sorry I'm late! I had an emergency!"

Flora breezed in and you had to try not to roll your eyes. She flopped on a couch between Onome and Fatima, and almost immediately started to cry. They cooed and fussed over her, and you almost laughed. You watched as she narrated—with dramatic hand gestures and a heaving bosom—that her husband wanted to leave her and move abroad with another man. Through her narration, you noticed that her makeup was flawless, and her face contoured to perfection. Despite her hysterics, there were no teardrops. The bitch was dead inside. You knew this because she was like you.

You always knew Flora was a hustler: after all, it took one to recognize one. You liked to think that you were a hustler with a conscience, while Flora was cold-blooded throughout. You'd met on the day of her wedding to Julius, one of Biodun's distant but maverick friends. It was one of those destination weddings, and it took place in Miami. You hadn't known anything about her at the time, so you were surprised when, during the dance when everyone sprayed money on the couple, she hugged you like a long-lost friend. Your first surprise was that you recognized her perfume and its price—Crab Apple Blossom by Clive Christian. Then she whispered, "Thanks for coming, Aunty mi. Sorry we're just meeting officially. I'll come and see you later because I know I'll need your help." Your face must have had a quizzical look because she leaned in again and whispered, "I'll need your help so I don't lose him to another man." You'd smiled but fumed inside because from her tone, she wasn't really asking for help—just letting you know she knew of the group. That was when you realized she was going to be a problem, and you immediately started thinking up a plan to neutralize her.

"So why does Julius say he wants to leave?" Onome asked.

"He says he wants to be in a society where he's free to be his authentic self." Flora sneered. "And that he's in love."

"Hmm. Hope you've secured the bag sha," Gbonju said.

Shamefaced, Flora bowed her head and muttered what you already knew. "No."

You knew that apart from some Birkins, her expensive wardrobe, and two cars, Flora had no real money or business of her own. If Julius left, she was at the mercy of his generosity or parsimony because they had no children, and she had no leverage to blackmail him since he'd be in a country where his sexuality was celebrated. Also, you now knew that

Julius had made her sign confidentiality and prenup agreements, and he had chosen Miami for the wedding because its post-marriage distribution laws favored him as the wealthier person if they got divorced. It was the price she paid for her hubris in knowingly contracting to be the wife-for-hire to a wealthy gay man, and for being the outsider in the group. You remembered times in the past when she'd mocked other women in the group with her eyes as they worried and complained about their men.

"Aunty mi," Flora called out to you.

You looked up from your nails. "Yes, Flora?"

"I need your help, Aunty. I don't want to lose him to another man."

You remembered her saying almost these same words on her wedding day, and with a cocky tone. You willed yourself not to smile. "What exactly do you want me to do, Flora?"

"I don't know, Aunty. Blackmail him for me?"

You frowned. "That's beneath me. Besides, it sounds like Julius doesn't care."

"Ah! What about to look for any dirt on his side-chick, for example, a sex tape? Or pay him off?"

You pretended to think about it for a moment. "It's a long shot but I may know someone. Let me make a call and see. Excuse me, ladies." You stood, pretended to scroll through your phone as you left the living room. You went to one of the bedrooms, sat on the bed, held your phone to your ear, and calmly whispered gibberish into it for a long time. Eventually, you came back out to the living room and took your seat.

You held Flora's eyes. "I have spoken to a gentleman and explained, erm, the delicacy of the situation. He says he can help, but if you want his help, you must accept two things—first, it's going to cost you ten thousand dollars in cash, fully paid upfront; and second, there's no guarantee he'll succeed."

"Who's he?"

"I know he's a private investigator of some sort, and he does some undercover work in Lagos's gay communities, so he prefers to be incognito. I don't know his name or anything else about him, and I have never actually met him, so I'm in the dark as much as you are. My only role, if you decide to use him, is to be the middleman for the money and messages." Then you shook your head, sighed, and put your hands up. "You know what? To be honest, I'd rather not be involved in these shadowy shenanigans and whatnot. Perhaps you should find help yourself."

"Ah, Aunty mi, only you can help me." In a flash, Flora was on her knees in front of you.

You sized her up for a moment before you said, "Get off your knees, Flora. It's unseemly." You shrugged and sighed wearily. "Okay, I'll help." You waited till she was back on her seat. "I suppose we'll get the ball rolling when you send me the cash?"

"Ifedayo."

"Yes, ma."

"What's this I hear about you and Julius planning to leave Nigeria together and live abroad? Was that the plan when I linked you up with him?"

Ifedayo looked down at his tapered trousers and pointy shoes. "No, ma. That was not the plan," he said softly. He was a beautiful man, baby-faced, lithe, caramel complexioned, with pearls for teeth. He was also twenty-nine—barely just young enough to still be a side-piece for Julius, who preferred them younger; and old enough to pass as a potential buyer of one of your For Sale properties if he wore a suit. He wore a suit today, and you met in the living room of one of your For Sale apartments in Ikoyi, just the two of you.

"So why the change of plan, then?"

He took a moment to answer. "We fell in love."

"Ha! You or Julius, or both of you?"

"Both of us, ma."

"Ah, love. That meddlesome thing. So, what's the exact plan? You go to the States, right?"

"Yes, ma."

"Let me guess. Miami?"

"Yes, ma. How did you know?"

"I know he has a house there for residency and tax purposes which I won't bore you with. But what will you do there, Ifedayo?"

He shrugged. "I don't know. Just chill with him?"

"You've been gay-for-pay for how long now—five years?"

"I'm gay now, ma. Fully."

"I see." You wanted to say: but you're only gay with one rich old man, but you didn't. Instead, you asked, "In these five years, Ifedayo, what have you gotten apart from your apartment, car, and clothes? Nice suit, by the way."

"I don't understand the question, ma."

"How much is in your account, Ifedayo?"

"About seven-fifty thousand naira, ma."

"So, after five years work, you have an apartment, a secondhand car, some secondhand clothes, seven hundred and fifty thousand naira, and a soft life. How long do you think this is going to last?"

"I don't understand, ma."

"Let me speak plainly as I see it. Julius has always preferred younger men, between nineteen and twenty-two. Yes, you met when you were twenty-five, but remember you have good genes and have always looked younger than you are. But good genes will only take you so far before age catches up. Julius may well love you now, but what if one day he stops, and trades you in for a younger piece. Have you seen the gorgeous offerings in Miami? I have."

You sighed. "My point is, you need to plan for your future. Here's my suggestion. Get admission for an MBA at a university in Miami, and get Julius to pay fully for it. By fully I mean tuition and board so you have a place to stay if you guys break up. If he refuses to pay, let me know, and I'll speak to him. That way, when you get to Miami, you'll have something else to do other than being Julius's trophy boyfriend, and you have a chance to stay behind, work, start a career, and build your life if things go pear-shaped. Am I clear?"

He nodded. "Thank you, ma."

"You're welcome. One more thing . . ." You opened your purse and pulled out the envelope containing Flora's ten thousand dollars. You handed it to him. "It's my goodbye gift. Promise me you won't spend it till you get to the States. When you get there, put more than half of it in an investment account. I'll give you the email of my financial adviser and he'll walk you through how to grow this money. Am I clear?"

There were sudden tears in his eyes. He shook his head. "Why are you doing all this for me, ma?"

You smiled. "Because someone did it for me and taught me how to thrive with the kind of men we both roll with." You patted his shoulder. "You're a lone wolf now. Act like it."

I KNEW YOU

Some things are easier to have than to hold on to, you get? Like wealth. Like friendship. Like love.

Finding love is easy. I'm not a bad-looking guy; I have my ways, my tricks. Women have always come, and they have gone. I'm easy to get, but not easy to tie down, you see. And all women, at some point, want a down payment. An assurance. Something concrete. A ring, a house . . . my last name. And that part, that last part, is the hard one for me.

Now I am haunted by ghosts and memories. Something inside me is broken, and nothing, not even the usual—drinks, pussy, even music! Man, my first love—can fix me.

The thing is, I don't even blame you. I wish I had the luxury of being bitter, or angry, anything but this fucking pain, this sense of loss. But I want you to know, I really don't blame you. It is funny how, when people ask why we are not together, I simply say that it's because I was afraid of losing you.

I remember the night we met.

I was the lead singer of the band performing that night at O'Jays. It's a small place, you get, but it has the right ambience. Proper music lovers come here, not just your usual Lagos fun seekers. You came in with your friends. You smelled of roses; I knew it was your smell because I leaned in as you walked by, but it was your excitement that held me. "Okay, that guy can sing!" You screamed so I could hear you. You thought your voice melted into the chatter. It didn't. I heard you. I had prepared a medley of songs but I knew the moment I saw you that I only wanted to sing for you.

"Guys, let's switch up this playlist. Give the ladies something a little bit more upbeat." I tried to sound laid-back as I appealed to the band, but I had my eye on you. I saw you and your friends find a table and order a batch of cocktails. I knew you were going to stick around for the night.

"Sid, you dey crase?" Tayo, my saxophonist, looked like he wanted to burst with anger or maybe just burst. Tayo was fat, but he didn't mind us making fun of him when we all hung out. The guy had a comeback for every diss. He was the sharp-mouthed clown of our posse.

"Please now, Tayo, I will give you my tips for the night." I'm a man of my word, so that was enough to have him growl in agreement. Money was Tayo's love language— money and food.

I started with Victor Uwaifo's "Mammy Water" then I

flowed into some Harry Belafonte. I didn't look at you for a while, but thirty minutes into the set, I gave up and I looked. Man, you were so beautiful. You would tell me later that when our eyes met, you felt dizzy. The only time you ever felt like that was moments before performing a surgery. It was a rush of adrenaline, then a wash of dizziness and then laser focus.

"So, you wanted to open me up? Kinky." I liked to tease you when we swapped stories. This particular joke ended when you left medicine for me. Even though you said you had no regrets. I know you would have been phenomenal if love hadn't interrupted your plans for life.

After my set, you came up to me.

"That was quite a performance," you said.

"Thank you. I was trying to impress you." I made my voice soft, raspy yet deep enough to create an effect that would enthrall you. It did. But I hate that you spoke to me first. I wish it had been me. I was still in my head trying to decide what I wanted to say. You were always the one who threw caution to the wind, you took major steps without hesitation.

We spoke for a few minutes but my mind kept trying to imagine how you would taste. Would the chapman you had been sipping on all night linger on your tongue? You licked your lips unconsciously—a habit you kept through our many phases together. You caught me looking at you.

"You want to kiss me, don't you?"

"Yes."

"Take me somewhere, then, and kiss me."

I took your hand and we left the crowd behind, edging into the darkness that was the back of O'Jays. We found a comfortable spot where I had your back against the wall, and then I leaned in to kiss you. I bit your lower lip and soothed it, slipped my tongue gently into your mouth, encouraging you to participate. You would later tell me that I tasted of mint and cigarettes, a flavor that made you so heady, you wanted more of it. When you opened up for me, I went deep; we made love to each other with our tongues while my hand traveled to your breasts and teased a nipple till it hardened beneath my touch. Reluctantly, I dragged my mouth from your lips and sought out the bud through your shirt and I sucked. You said your knees nearly gave out from the sensation that shot through you, and you were glad you weren't wearing a padded bra. I moved from one breast to the other, sucking, teasing. Fuck. You were so soft. I ground your butt hard and pushed you against my throbbing member, so you felt the extent of my desire.

Tayo burst through the back door just then, like a literal bull in a china shop, looking for God knows what. We pulled apart and laughed like we were drunk on champagne.

I would have fucked you right there at O'Jays, but I knew

you didn't deserve that. Years later, you told me you would not have minded.

Here's the thing.

I was full of myself. Not like I thought I was special, not like that, I'm personally just an okay guy. What I mean is, I thought that life gives you innumerable chances. Stupid, right? I really thought that if one lane doesn't work out, you can just find another one. If a girl breaks your heart, get another one to fix it. That kind of thing. I knew you were special from the moment we met, that this was different from what I was used to. But I thought meeting you was the beginning of greater things. Maybe since I experienced love with you, I could always re-create it with someone else if we didn't work out. The universe is a sneaky motherfucker, though. You were it. That night was it. And I blew it.

Let me try to describe how I see you, in a little more detail.

When you walk into a room, it's as if you're giving the cold shoulder to a crowd of haters. You embody a type of grace, the way you carry yourself—soft but edgy. My favorite thing about your beauty is your silhouette, that long, elegant neck. Like a ballerina, or a swan. You're kind of rare, babe. Your type is really scarce, I knew that then, and I know it now. But the sweet thing was, you let down that guard with me completely. It was such a turn-on.

Man, I love that about you—your shamelessness, as you often call it. I knew you were only that way around me. How could I have taken such a thing for granted?

A week after we met, we made love for the first time. In my one-bedroom apartment, a converted boys' quarter in Ikoyi where an acquaintance was letting me stay rent-free. A live version of Fela's "V.I.P." was playing in the background. In those days, I used to keep my record player at the edge of the mattress, beside the standing fan with its blades moving in lazy circles because the power supply fluctuated. Our sweaty bodies had moved in harmony with the rhythm of the song until we climaxed together. You looked beautiful with your hair sticking to your forehead and your shift dress bunched up around your waist. You are the only woman I can bear to look in the eyes as we fuck. I watched the plea-sure mount in your eyes, saw them glisten just before you came and you had to squeeze them shut. Right then a song lyric popped into my head—it would become the first line of my first hit song.

As we lay naked, wrapped up in each other, analyzing ev-ery moment since we met, you told me I was your second and last. I didn't want that kind of pressure, so I distracted you by singing. You said my voice was a balm you would always need.

Sometimes when the alcohol doesn't drown out memories of you, I can still hear you asking me to make you mine. My response never changes even in the trances I have of you. I always say, let us see how it goes.

I am afraid, even in my dreams, of losing you.

You are the smart one, the doctor, so I thought you would know. It was there from the start, from the very first phone conversation we had. That was the fascinating thing about us, we went hard and deep so quickly, it didn't even feel scary at first. No, wait, that's a lie. I was always fucking scared but I liked being with you, listening to you talk, and everything else so much that it overrode the fear.

It was always there. Didn't you sense it?

That night after we kissed at O'Jays, I waited four hours to call you. I didn't want to seem desperate after we exchanged numbers, you get. No woman had ever aroused me like that but I knew we were going to be more so I had to rein it in.

When I called, you answered on the third ring.

"Hey, this is Sid. Can you talk?"

"Hi, Rusty!"

You sounded sexy even on the phone. Especially on the phone, you have a voice made for phone sex, babe. That night I wanted to try my luck to nudge you into a steamy conversation, but then you had to go all deep on me.

"Rusty? What's that about?" I asked.

"Have you never seen a mirror? You have reddish hair, I meant to ask about that. Is it natural?"

"Sort of."

"Are you oyibo or something?"

"I'm as Yoruba as you are."

"Is it some kind of genetic anomaly, then?"

"It's from my dad's side."

"Oh. So you are a little bit oyibo."

"Not oyibo, Arab. He's Algerian."

"Interesting. Do you look like him?"

"Nope, I am my mother's son. Apart from the hair, and maybe my nose."

"Well, I like your hair and nose, Sid. Is that your real name?"

"Sadiq. The guys thought I needed a stage name."

"I like it."

"Is there anything about me you don't like?" I said, laughing.

"I didn't like that you stopped kissing me."

"I didn't want to." My voice went two octaves lower. My dick was hard just hearing you speak.

"Are we going to do it again?"

"Fuck, yes."

This time it was you who laughed.

"I'll look forward to it, Sadiq."

"Not too forward, we can meet tomorrow. I'm free, where do you live?"

"Can't for a week, I have surgeries."

"You're a doctor?"

"Just a baby one. Two years into it."

"Where do you work?"

"This week I'll be at LASUTH. But I move around a bit."

"Cool. So it's a deal. I'll see you next week."

Not proud of this, but after I ended the call your voice stayed with me even as I wanked off with Onome on the phone. I climaxed to the thought of you. It was the last time I had phone sex with another woman.

Before we met again, we spent hours on the phone talking about everything and nothing. I want to call you now but I know you would never answer, and even if you did, that special joy in your voice would no longer be there.

A month after we met, people stopped saying, "Sid, how far?" and started saying, "Sid, how your babe?" That was a lot for me. To tell you the truth, the only thing I knew about love before you was that it ends. That's it. Happy endings are for mumus and fairy tales. Happy endings are the code name for a special type of massage in brothels. When it comes to relationships, you're lucky if you get a happy beginning and a not-so-terrible ending.

I had walked life alone before you, and in the blink of an eye you had become the yin to my yang. It was a lot. This is why I never claimed you. I never put a tag on us because I didn't want to scare myself. It was never about you. I know you hated the fact that you were the one who always had to add "girlfriend" whenever I made the introductions. But I gave you everything else. Everything that a man like me has to give. Why wasn't that enough?

Three months after that first kiss, you told me you loved me. I don't know how you missed the fear in my eyes. Maybe it was because NEPA had robbed us of electricity that night as usual, so you couldn't see my face clearly in the moonlit darkness of that room.

Four months after we first made love, we moved in together. You left your job and started freelancing with a tele-medicine firm based in South Africa. I moved out of the BQ and we got a place in Surulere, a few streets away from O'Jays. Six months into it, the band and I went on our first tour around Lagos. The headline song was the one I wrote for you. We got our first major deal on that tour; you made sure to attend every stop as the dutiful girlfriend.

A few days after the tour ended, I sat with you at your

family's weekly get-together. I was finally able to make one of the many family outings you had invited me to. Even though I was late and the food was finished, you were grateful I came.

I remember saying to you that I felt warm inside seeing how your parents still loved each other despite the fact that they had spent nearly three decades together. I remember the genuine love I saw in your father's eyes when you introduced us. Your mother's hug made my eyes water but I hid it well. I kept looking for something that would tick me off. Your sister, Tolu, and two brothers, Tayo and Tife, and their partners were throwing bants and even threw some at me. I was laughing but I knew I never wanted that kind of love. It was too open. Like outer space, like the ocean, endless, without boundaries; so open that I knew getting lost in it was a certainty. And I never want to do that—lose myself to anything.

That is why I never went with you to your parents' ever again.

Let me make it clear that I'm not a guy with "issues." I am actually very simple, I'm sure you can tell. Complicated doesn't describe me at all. What I am, though, is a person with lived experience. A person who has seen things. A person who believes what they know to be true over what-ever else people might try to sell them. You can't hustle me into buying your version of reality.

But I'm trying, I'm really trying to unlearn some of these traits that have led me here. I know I never said much about my father. Let me tell you about him—the bastard. The first thing you should know is that I don't hate him. You have to know somebody to hate them. I don't know that guy. I met him like three times in total, and the last two times, I had to keep him off my mum, you get.

That day at your parents' house, you said, "Don't mind them. They keep acting like they are newlyweds. That is why Tolu and her husband feel comfortable making out in front of us all."

You rolled your eyes as if you were irritated, but the tiny smile and the lightness I heard in your voice told me how happy you were.

"It's really cool, jare. Leave them alone. Thank you again for inviting me."

I put my arm around your shoulder as we watched your sister's children play hide-and-seek in the garden of your parent's Ikoyi townhouse.

I was lying through my teeth, babe. For some people ly-ing is a coping mechanism, a survival tactic. After my mother died, my father never came back from France, never called. As far as I know he has another family over there. The best I can hope for is that he isn't fucking them over like he did me and my mum.

I was all alone from age sixteen. Before she died, all my mother did was work hard and complain. She told me that my father only made her happy for three months. All that hardship in exchange for three happy months. They met by chance. My mother was a young waitress at a high-end hotel. He was visiting Nigeria with his family. They should have ignored whatever attraction they felt. Instead, they took it too far, and crashed and burned. I'm not angry with either of them; they fell for the scam that love lasts or means something. Besides, my mother was truly good to me, she gave me everything she had to give.

Layo, people like me can't give you what your parents have. It's not in my DNA. The only instinct I have is knowing exactly when to cut and run. The rest of the time, I'm just winging it.

In the first two years we "broke up" maybe five times. The first time was when you noticed I had never said I love you. You looked at me, your toothbrush in your hand and a mouth full of foam. I used that as an excuse to pretend I hadn't heard what you said. You spat with force into the sink and repeated yourself.

"I said, why have you never said you love me?"

"What is obvious doesn't need to be said, babe. I have a whole song that I sing two hundred nights a year saying how much you mean to me. How many women in this town can say that?"

"It's just three little words. I say it all the time to you, why can't you say it back? Don't you think I deserve to hear it too?"

"I just don't think it's a big deal, you get?"

"You won't say it?"

"You've put too much of a spotlight on it. Now I'm shy."

I thought you would crack a smile, instead you packed up a small bag and left. I lasted three days before I came begging. It took another week before I squeezed the words out of my throat. I hugged you tight and whispered them in your ear. When you melted into my arms and fell against me, I wondered why I hadn't said it sooner.

We fought and made up. We were good friends and better lovers. You liked me so much I had no choice but to start liking myself, to start acting respectable, like someone who had something special waiting for them back home.

The last two times we broke up I was the one who did it.

On the first occasion I came home to our flat and met it in semi-darkness. There were tea lights everywhere and John Coltrane was playing in the background. You always said his music made you think of me, the way you felt about me. When I found you in the bedroom, you were wearing my PJs as you liked to do, your smaller feet in my larger slides. You handed me a gift bag.

Man.

It's obscene for a person to feel the kind of horror that I did despite the mood you had set. The present was a positive pregnancy test.

Because I am a good actor, I faked the kind of joy I knew you would like to see. I held you that night as you peacefully slept, my eyes red-rimmed and wide open with terror.

The next morning, I faked an impromptu gig, disappeared to a small motel in Ikeja for two days, and drowned myself in alcohol. What did I know of fatherhood, man? I didn't have one of those, ever. Did I want to pass whatever messed-up genes I had to some poor unsuspecting soul? Fuck that. I ran and was going to stay running but Tayo found me. For a guy that size he's stealthy and very sneaky. He tracked my phone o, said he knew some guy that did stuff like that.

When he saw me at the door, I thought he might slap me but then he shook his head in pity.

"You be small pikin? How can you lie about a gig and not tell your bandmates first? Ode."

When I didn't respond, he continued. "Better go and baff and return to Layo before I sit on you. Fool."

At this point I started laughing. Tayo joined in too, clapping me on my shoulder with undue force as he said, "Congratulations, my guy."

June 6, 2015. The first time I remember ever crying. Not even my mum's death or you leaving me did that. The day I saw Tomisin for the first time. She was perfect.

She looked just like you.

These days when I call, Tomisin often tells me you are not home. I never thought you would be the kind of mother to leave her two children with the nanny to go partying. That was okay six years ago when we met, not anymore. You once told me that you had no reason to go out at night because you had found me. Why are you going out at night now? I am still here.

After we had Tomi, our love changed a little bit. It matured. Or rather, you matured. Motherhood looked so good on you. I'm older but you have always been wiser. I was so scared of being a dad but once I learned to follow your lead it was easy. And she was a good baby. A gig baby, ha, that poor child was in bars and clubs from six months old. You found these cute baby-sized earmuffs that reduce noise, and on nights she was around it was strictly nonsmoking. By the time she was two and her brother, Tobi, was born, she could sing along to some of our songs.

Layo, you were my good luck charm. We had a real family. I moved us into a bigger house. A duplex with a spare room for guests. We ate dinner together and went to the beach on weekends when I wasn't on tour. We had a real family and we were so happy.

I still can't believe you had to go and ruin it with another surprise.

I should have felt it coming. It had been a month since your parents came to visit us, one of the few times I was home from touring. We received them happily but their tongues did a lot of damage.

You had thrown them a party to celebrate their twenty-five-year marriage anniversary. I was thoughtful enough to have given you the money to plan it. I didn't complain when you left the tour early. I showed up to support and celebrate them. Everything was perfect.

As the evening wound down, they escorted their guests out and then your parents decided to drop a bomb before leaving.

"Thank you for this wonderful party," your mother said quietly.

"You are welcome, Mummy," we responded.

"May God continue to fill your hearts with laughter," your father prayed.

"Amen."

"By this time next year, we will be gathering to celebrate your official union and many other things," your father continued.

Dead silence.

"Amen!"

You yelled loud enough to make my silence not noticeable.

It didn't work.

They quickly rounded off the prayer, your mother pulled both of us into a hug, and they left. That night, for the first time in our relationship, you didn't sleep a wink. I know because I was awake too. I tried to distract you by making love to you the next morning.

It didn't work.

"Do you see us getting married?" you asked the moment I rolled off you.

Dead silence.

"Why are you asking?"

"That is not an answer. Answer the question." Dead silence.

"I don't know . . . I guess."

"When?"

Dead silence.

"Let's see how this year goes."

That answer obviously didn't satisfy you, because you proposed a month later at Tobi's birthday party.

That was not fair to me.

Things were fine at first, at the party. Our little man waddled into the converted living room in his little agbada, complete with the abeti aja fila. Everyone swooned. We were so proud as he chased the balloons and everyone clapped and made merry. After we cut the cake, the party started winding down so that the adults could get their groove on. My band was there, your parents, siblings, and our friends were present. The adults were finally able to have fun since the kids were being managed by the maids upstairs.

"Tobi looks so much like Sadiq! He even has the same atarodo hair color," I heard your sister say as I walked past you to get drinks.

I didn't catch your response but laughter, joy, and endless chatter filled the room. An hour into the drinking and eating fest, Tayo, who was now my road manager, made a joke.

"Sid, when will you marry Layo naw? I for marry her but my last name no sweet like your own. Omolayo Bensaïd. That name sweet die to call," he said.

Nervous laughter trickled through the room but the mood had changed. Don't worry, I have fired that court jester. He won't embarrass us like that again.

"Uncle Tayo, help me ask him. So, when will you make an

honest woman out of me?" you asked once the room became calm again.

All eyes were on us. I still can't believe you made us the center of attention for no reason.

"Sadiq Bensaïd, when will you marry me?" you asked again.

I pleaded with you with my eyes to drop it but you sat resolutely across the table looking at me. No one said anything. Everywhere was quiet and the silence lasted three fucking minutes. I was looking at the wall clock the whole time. Do you know how long three minutes is? Silence became a sound, like a hum in my ear. That's how long the three minutes it took to break up with you felt. It defied physics. It froze time.

Then you got up and thanked everyone for coming, wished them a good evening; within an hour, our home was empty but the silence lingered. I was still in the same position another hour later when you returned from putting the children to bed.

"This is not working anymore. When you go on tour tomorrow, don't come back here. Find a place to rent close by so that the children can adjust to the new arrangement."

I wanted to laugh.

What?

Who leaves a man they love because of a ring? Who deprives their children, a two-year-old, for godsakes, of their dad for that reason? When he's older and he asks you why you left me, can you really tell him why?

That was six months ago. I haven't been the same since. I quit the tour with three shows to go because I was a mess. The blogs and social media chatter were brutal. They said I had lost my touch. My voice was in shambles. I was soaked in alcohol all the time and my vision was blurry. I don't know how you're feeling, I think that's the other thing that really hurts. You were so cold that night, you seemed so sure. And the two times I have called to speak to you, you have sounded the same. Could I have lost you? I can't have lost you, right?

Yesterday, I recorded a new song for you. I tried to say what my silence and running away couldn't say. Marriage destroys love, in my experience. I never wanted to gamble what we have by taking us down that route. I wanted to stay still. I wrote this one last song for you to let you know that I'm waiting for you. You are my home, and I'm hoping you come back to me.

INDEPENDENCE DAY

On what you would ordinarily consider a perfect day, you ran into the man who raped you.

Usually, you loved early-October days like these. The rainy season was ending, the dry one was about to start. Last night's rains gifted a soothing cool to today. The sky held no clouds and wore its purest blue. And though the sun was bright, it gave no heat and, strangely, reminded you of the flawless sunny-side-up eggs Lekan, your husband, usually made for you.

You saw your rapist at your seven-year-old son's school. It turned out that his son and yours were classmates, and you'd met his wife, Funke, many times during school runs. It was only when she turned up with her husband in tow today because of the school's Cultural Day, you realized how supremely fucked up some of life's coincidences were.

October 1 is Nigeria's Independence Day. The school's

yearly Cultural Day was always held on this day because it was a public holiday, and more parents could attend. Typically, on previous Cultural Days, the school grouped the children into the three main Nigerian tribes of Hausa, Yoruba, and Igbo, and asked the children to turn up in the traditional outfits of those three. However, this year, you had reminded Mrs. Nwokedi, the head teacher, that Nigeria had more than three hundred tribes, and perhaps it was time for others to get a look-in. So, for Cultural Day this year, the children were allowed to wear the outfit of any tribe they chose. You expected Lekan Jr. to choose to wear the dashiki and fila of your husband's Yoruba people, but you were pleasantly surprised when he said he wanted to dress as a Bini man to represent yours. You and Lekan had fun sourcing the appropriate outfit, and dressing Lekan Jr. in the ebuluku, the white cloth around his waist and draped over his left shoulder, the coral beads over his neck and on his wrists— you even got him a traditional horsetail fan, which he kept waving with exaggerated magnificence.

The cruel coincidence was, Charles raped you on October 1, sixteen years ago.

You were stunned when you recognized Charles with Funke and their son, Jayden, in the school's courtyard just before the start of Cultural Day. Funke smiled and waved at you, as she usually did, and you would have returned the greeting or even exchanged brief hugs. But Charles was there. And your world had suddenly been upended. And time had stopped.

From the furtive look in his eyes, you knew Charles had recognized you. You wanted to scream and pull your hair, then lunge at Charles. You wished Lekan was here with you because he would know what to do—he had planned to attend, but the hospital where he worked as a cardiovascular surgeon had called him in this morning to perform an emergency surgery. You barely managed to control yourself enough to look Charles in the eye and say a cold hello to Funke without breaking eye contact with him. He looked away. Lekan Jr. wriggled and shook his hand in discomfort, and you realized that you'd been squeezing his hand too tightly. Funke's eyes widened, and her brows were raised in a puzzled look. You mumbled a hasty goodbye and walked past them, tugging Lekan Jr. into the school area.

Your heart beat so violently, it felt like it was about to tear out of your chest. You took a deep breath to hold back the sudden tears—and you remembered the times you told yourself, promised yourself, that you'd cried enough over Charles.

Mrs. Nwokedi saw you and made her way over through the crowd. You knew she came to remind you that you'd give a short speech on behalf of the parents, after the children's presentations. You smiled at her but didn't hear a word of what she said because though your body was there, your mind had time-traveled.

How did you let yourself became acquaintances with
Funke? You tried to replay every conversation you'd had with
her at the car park or the parents' waiting area during school
runs. "My husband is never around! I swear, I married a non-
existent person," she'd half-joked once. "You know how busy
some men are," you'd replied. "Sometimes, we just have to
support them by carrying on when they're not around."
She'd touched your shoulder, smiled stiffly, and said, "Thank
you, Osa."

How could you not have noticed till today that Jayden had
Charles's eyes, and mouth, and the same square-shaped face?
The apple usually never fell far from the tree, you thought,
and you felt a sudden irrational hatred for the boy as you
imagined him growing up to be a rapist like his father.

"Mummy, are you okay?" your son asked.

You exhaled heavily and nodded. Then you bent to his
level and asked, seriously, "Tell me the truth—does Jayden
touch girls in school?"

"Jayden? Touch girls?"

"Yes! Answer me. Has he ever touched their bums or
kissed them?"

He frowned. "No, Mummy."

"Are you sure?"

"Yes, Mummy. Why will he do that?"

"You know what, Junior? Forget about it, okay?"

He nodded.

"But promise me one thing. Promise me you will stop being friends with Jayden. Promise?" You offered him your right pinkie.

He scowled. "He's not really my friend, but why?"

You sighed. "You won't understand now. Just trust me, and promise me, okay?"

"Okay," he mumbled reluctantly as he locked his pinkie with yours. "I promise."

That day was perfect too.

You were seventeen, fresh out of secondary school. You had exceled in your JAMB exam and gotten admission to study architecture in Unilag. School hadn't started yet due to the usual ASUU strikes, so you spent the time interning at a business center owned by one of your father's friends. But you didn't go to work that day.

Aunty Philo, your father's sister, saw you in bed that morning and asked, "Osariemen, no work today?"

"Aunty, today is public holiday."

"And so? Get up. As your papa no dey house, follow me to my shop."

Philo had moved in three years ago, after your mum died. The idea was that she'd provide some type of maternal care since your father didn't know how to cope with two children on his own. Fourteen-year-old you had resisted the idea and had told your father that you were independent and could take care of Usifo, your younger brother, who was eleven at the time and just started boarding school. You'd also reminded your father that your late mother and Aunty Philo didn't like each other—the unspoken implication being that Philo's presence would be a slight on your mother's memory. But your father hadn't listened.

As you expected, after she moved in, Aunty Philo was cantankerous, regularly made snide remarks about your mother, and was more concerned with running her provisions shop, which your father opened for her. Naturally, you butted heads, and you tried to avoid her as much as possible.

"Aunty, I already have somewhere to go to. My oga at work sent me on an errand." It was an obvious lie, but you didn't care. You'd decided you weren't going with her to her shop. Having lied, you needed to get out of the house, and away from her for a few hours.

That was when you remembered Charles, a guy from your Yaba neighborhood. He'd been asking you to date him for a while, and to be honest, you were considering it. He wasn't much to look at, but he was a third-year student at UI, sounded passionate and intelligent when he talked about societal injustices and the upcoming revolution of the masses, and most important, he was the most consistent of all your toasters. Lately, you'd been thinking maybe the time was right to finally have a boyfriend, after years of promising yourself that boys would wait till you got into university.

You remembered that Charles had sent you a message yesterday asking you if you were available to hang out with him today. So you picked your phone and sent him a text:

Hi Charles, I am free today if you want to hang out. Happy Independence Day.

He responded ten minutes later:

Yes! Finally! Lol. Can I pick you up at 1 and we go to that new fast food place close to your house?

You replied:

Yes.

You showered, made up as best as you knew how, and wore your favorite casual maxi summer dress. He showed up an hour late claiming he had to go drop his friends off at the airport. You were all too eager to leave the house, you didn't press it when he drove past the fast-food restaurant.

"Oh, sorry. Impromptu change of plans. Some of my friends are having a small party in Festac. I just want to breeze in, show my face, and leave."

"I have to be back home by six and it is already two."

"Don't worry. We'll be back by then. I promise."

You spent almost two hours in traffic. Even then, he was apologetic. "I'm sorry, Osa. I didn't expect this much traffic on a public holiday. Lagos is always crazy. Don't worry, we'll just stay for five minutes then head back. I'll get you home by six."

"It's cool," you said, but it really wasn't. The midday heat had turned up several notches, and the air-conditioning in his car was bad. What made the ride bearable was he played a lovely selection of hits—from "African Queen" to "Bizzy Body," "Nwa Baby," "Drop It Like It's Hot," "Olufunmi," "Tongolo," and "Road to Zion." The music in the car carried you as he drove into the heart of Festac and stopped in front of an apartment block from where another source of music boomed. You smiled when he opened the door for you to get down, and took your hand to lead you in.

You paused before you went in. "We're only staying for a moment, right?"

"Yes. Ten minutes tops."

You smiled, but mentally, you gave yourself an hour to stay.

The party was in full swing as you entered with him. He pulled you into a circle of his friends, and you liked that he introduced you as his future girlfriend. His friends and their girlfriends seemed like a good-natured bunch, just a little raucous.

You didn't remember how everyone started playing Truth or Dare. It was your first time playing and there was no way you were going to tell your secrets to strangers, even if they were older university students you regarded as cool. So, when they dared you to, you kissed Charles, to the cheers and whoops of his friends. It was your first kiss, but you'd seen how it was done on TV. You remembered thinking he was a bad kisser because his tongue was unwieldy like a brick in your mouth, and his breath was stale.

When you looked at your watch and saw that your hour was up, you told him you wanted to go home.

"Soon. Relax."

You let him be and mentally prepared yourself for the verbal war that would ensue between you and Aunt Philo.

Then he handed you a drink. "I got you this. I know you don't take alcohol. But this is punch." He watched you intently as you took a sip. You were thirsty, and it was cold and sweet. You gulped it all down. He smiled.

When you suddenly began to feel groggy and the walls swayed and danced, he leaned in and his breath blew heat in your ear as he whispered, "Come, let's go somewhere quiet." You remember realizing something was wrong, and things were about to get worse. You wanted to say no as he pulled you, but your tongue felt glued to the floor of your mouth and a dark fog enveloped you.

Your next memory, still hazy, was being with him in a

dark, messy room. You lay on your back on a bed, half-hypnotized by the blades of a whirring fan. His weight crushed you, and you felt almost disembodied as he kissed and groped you. You tried to push him off, but your limbs were as heavy as tree trunks. The pull to close your eyes and drift again was strong. You closed your eyes but felt dull stings on your face. You struggled to open your eyes, and saw his face contorted in a grimace of disgust as he slapped you. You felt his other hand tug at your underwear. Your heart sank as he rolled your dress up your thighs easily.

You summoned all your strength and willpower to try to move. You managed to lift a heavy hand and weakly, tried to push him away.

You saw him frown, lift his arm above his shoulder. You realized he was going to slap you the exact moment he did. A bomb exploded in your head and scattered what felt like nuts and bolts and broken pieces. At the same time, you saw what looked like fireworks just before you blacked out.

When you came to, your head was ringing but also making no sound. His trousers were off now, and he wore just his gray T-shirt with the dark sweat rings at his arm-pits. You watched him use his knees to pin your legs apart. He tried to shove his erect penis into you, but he couldn't because you were dry. After three unsuccessful pokes, he pulled away slightly, and used a thumb to rub the pre-seminal fluid over the head of his penis to get lubrication.

He poked you again but still couldn't get it in. He glared accusatorily at you, and you so feared he was going to hit you again, you were prepared to plead with him that it wasn't really your fault your body didn't know how to respond because you were a virgin.

You saw the lightbulb come on in his head. He pulled away slightly again, and worked his jaws maniacally. When he built up a considerable glob of saliva, he spat in his hand and used it to vigorously stroke his penis. He repeated the process three times till it glistened with a wet and messy sheen. He was ready.

This time, it worked. You screamed as he tore into you. Quickly, he clamped his palm over your nose and mouth. It smelled of his saliva and bad breath. As he began to rock on top of you, he also pawed at and bit your breasts. He'd squished your dress way up to your neck, and it felt like a noose. And with his hand over your face, you realized you couldn't breathe. You didn't want to breathe. You wanted to die. You prayed to die. You let your body go limp and waited to die.

But you didn't die.

Instead, you felt his body tremble. Then he pulled out of you, pulled off you, grunted, spasmed, and spurted a dribble of warm sperm down your thighs. That was when you noticed your tears had rolled down the side of your face.

You closed your eyes and slept because you wished it was

a dream, and maybe from dreams, you could slip through a door to death.

But you didn't die.

You had to endure the long ride home with him from Festac, since you hadn't come out with enough money because the original plan had been to go to the new fast-food place down your street in Yaba. You huddled in a corner of the car, as far away from him as possible, silent, and zombied out. He said he did it because you took too long to agree to be his girlfriend, especially after he'd spent money on dates with you. You didn't speak, but you recalled it was three dates—you hadn't ordered anything on the first, you'd had just a Coke on the second, and a Coke and one meat pie on the third. He said he wanted to see you again. He didn't apologize, but said he'd be gentler next time.

Maybe there was something about your face and the way you shuffled into the house that night, but Aunty Philo didn't shout at you as you'd expected her to. And from then, she just let you be—though many times afterward, you caught her staring at you intently, as though she could sense that something in you had been irreparably broken.

You went straight to the bathroom and scrubbed yourself

raw. Afterward, you started bathing three or four times a day. But you never felt clean enough.

Charles called the next day, but you didn't answer. He sent texts saying he wanted to talk, but you didn't reply. You blocked his number. Eventually, you changed your phone number and cut off from everyone.

You never drank Coke or ate meat pie again. It was all for the best, you bitter-joked to yourself, since a man raped you because of two Cokes and a meat pie.

You stopped wearing makeup and dresses. You turned to baggy tops and jeans to hide your figure. You wore extra shorts over your underwear and under your jeans, and hard-to-unbuckle belts to make it harder for the next man who could try to rape you.

You decided you'd kill the next man who tried. By then, you'd become an architecture student and X-Acto knives were part of your tools for school. So you always carried a set of knives in your bag (even after you graduated). Luckily, you didn't kill anyone, though you once caused a scene at Yaba Market when you slashed the hand of one of those notorious street traders who'd groped you.

You always ensured you had vex money with you, but it was useless because you never dated. You never went to parties either.

You stopped being able to sleep for more than four hours each day. After some years, you tried drinking every night, hoping to get some sleep. But alcohol didn't work for you. You only started sleeping normally when Usifo gave you some sleeping pills. At the time, he was training to be a pharmacist and interning at the pharmacy of a private hospital during his holidays. Eventually, you asked for stronger pills as your body got used to the earlier ones. Eventually, Usifo, the closest person to you since your mother died, asked what was wrong with you.

So you told him. Six years after it happened.

It was Usifo who, after he'd cried with you, started giving you antidepressants along with the sleeping pills.

Then he got caught. It turned out he'd been stealing the pills from the hospital's pharmacy, and he'd never told you.

The hospital was a private one, owned and run by two generations of a close-knit family of doctors—made up of siblings, cousins, and their adult children (one of whom was Lekan). Because he liked Usifo and had taken him under his wing, he used his influence to ensure that the hospital only fired Usifo but didn't report him to the police or his university (so as not to jeopardize his career as a pharmacist). Somehow, privately, he also got Usifo to admit he stole the drugs for you, because he believed you were suffering PTSD from a traumatic event (Usifo never told him about the rape).

And that was how Lekan, who'd never seen or met you, offered to pay for your sessions with the hospital's psychiatrist and for any prescribed drugs.

And that was how you met Lekan—at the hospital when you came for your sessions.

Lekan who instinctively treated everyone with an amazing kindness. Lekan with his contagious smile and unruly laugh. Lekan the gregarious, funny, and mischievous. Lekan who had the audacity to live with the biggest heart, confident that he'd never let life or Nigeria break it permanently. Looking back, you realized he was possibly the only person who could have breached your walls, because of his personality and because he did it so smoothly, you didn't notice.

First, he waited for all your sessions to be completed. By then, you felt safe with him enough to develop a friendship of sorts despite the twelve-year age gap.

Then he started inviting you to what you now regard as dates, though they never felt that way at the time. They were always people-filled or family events like christenings, barbecues, and Sunday lunches. They were also many simple watch-TV-in-a-group events at his house for English Premier League and Champions League football, Netflix movies and series, *Big Brother* evictions and finale.

You knew something had shifted when one day you asked Aunty Philo for her eyeliner and lip balm ointment because you were going to watch *Breaking Bad* at Lekan's house with him and his cousins. It had been years since you wore makeup, so you no longer kept any. You caught the end of her smile as she handed you the pencil and tin. That was when you realized you liked Lekan, and it disconcerted you so much.

At his house, there was a moment when it was just the two of you in his kitchen, trying to get more dishes and glasses. Suddenly, you blurted, "You know I'm still damaged, right?"

"You know that doesn't matter to me, right?" He smiled and passed you a plate without breaking stride.

You both joined the group in the living room. And sometime during the evening, you found yourself sitting next to him. And you slipped your hand in his. And you interlocked fingers like it was the most natural thing. And it felt good. And you felt that, maybe, tomorrow could be all right.

Two years later you married him. Nine years of marriage and a seven-year-old son later, he still looked at you like you were the prize.

And at some point in the middle of it all, you became glad you didn't die.

You thought about death today.

Specifically, you thought about killing Charles. He was with Funke two rows behind you in the school auditorium. You felt he'd chosen to sit behind you to avoid your stare. Still, he wasn't far, just a few feet away. You still carried an

X-Acto knife in your handbag, and you fancied yourself to get two or three stabs in his neck before they overpowered you. But you would never go back home, never raise your son, never love your husband, if you did.

Mrs. Nwokedi's voice interrupted your thoughts. "On behalf of the management and staff of the school, I'd like to thank all the parents and guests who turned up and participated in our Cultural Day. In particular, I'd like to thank one of our parents, Mrs. Osa Akindele, whose suggestion it was to make this year's Cultural Day more inclusive. She was also very supportive with her thoughtful and practical ideas, which made the event more fun and successful. I know she'd prefer to be in the background, but I feel it is only right to call on her to say a few words on behalf of the parents. Please put your hands together and give a warm welcome to Mrs. Osa Akindele."

They clapped as you walked to the podium. You didn't have a prepared speech for this, but you had a few talking points. It was going to be short.

They handed you the microphone. Mrs. Nwokedi hugged you and murmured something to you, but you couldn't hear her due to the deafening ringing in your head and pounding of your heart. You noticed, though, that your hand was steady.

"Thank you, Mrs. Nwokedi. Good afternoon, everyone. As we celebrate our country's independence, diversity, and complexities today, it is important to understand that every people and everyone should be allowed the time and space to express themselves, to vent, to tell their stories. Maybe after all that, we can then begin our national and individual journeys to respect, empathy, healing, and unity?" You shrugged.

"Speaking of stories, I have one to tell. I apologize in advance because ideally, I shouldn't tell you all this. But by a twist of fate, I find myself in an extraordinary situation, where, God help me, I have to speak."

You took a deep breath. "Sixteen years ago, a man drugged, beat, and raped me. I couldn't talk about it for a long time, but I just saw him here, and ah, Osanobua, I must talk."

You pointed at him. "Charles Adesulure! I'm now ready to talk about what you did to me. Charles, stop hiding behind your innocent wife, and look at me when I'm talking to you. You don't want to talk again, ehn, Charles? Where are you going, Charles? I just want to talk. Why are you running? Why are you running?"

ACKNOWLEDGMENTS

First, I want to thank all the women whose stories inspire me every day.

Special gratitude to Professor Olorode, I love you. My deepest gratitude to Eniola and Dunni—the best friends a girl could be so lucky to have. Thank you for holding me as I cried my eyes out after a mad man tried to break me. Thank you for always cheering me on, I am grateful for you.

I must thank my good friend Stanley Osi, whose kind words and patience helped me on days I had forgotten to believe in myself. You are special, Stan.

To Captain, there was a time you could capture everything in words. Those memories linger, thank you. This book is for your children, the ones I have met and will meet. I love them fiercely. Time has changed nothing.

Many thanks to Chimeka Garricks for mentoring me on this journey, and for the brilliant edits—I am and will always be a fan. And to Tahirah Sagaya, for all the time and effort you put into the manuscript, for making my writing sparkle. Thank you. Special thanks to Chimamanda Ngozi Adichie, who told me when I was sixteen at one of the readings for

Half of a Yellow Sun that I should take all my time to write my first book. I hope she reads this book and it makes her proud.

I have to thank my late aunty Professor Foluke Ogunleye, who never failed to cheer me on; continue to rest with the angels, Aunty, I miss you.

I would like to thank my wonderful editor, Gretchen Schmid, and the team at HarperCollins for making me feel seen all through the editing process. Special thanks, also, to Mark Richards of Swift Press and to Charlotte Seymour, who helped to make my work easier!

Many thanks to my mother, Oluremi, the backbone that never breaks. Maami, you are my hero. Kare iya mi, Abake, e kpe fun wa o. Amin.

No one has walked this path with me longer than God, and he will continue to walk it with me. I thank Him for everything I am. He is my everything. He is my life.

Here ends Damilare Kuku's
Nearly All the Men in Lagos Are Mad.

The first edition of this book was printed
and bound at Lakeside Book Company
in Harrisonburg, Virginia, February 2024.

A NOTE ON THE TYPE

The text of this book is set in Dante, a typeface designed in the mid-1950s by Giovanni Mardersteig, a well-known printer and designer who operated a private press called Officina Bodoni, and Charles Malin, a punch-cutter who hand-cut the original typeface before it was adapted for mechanical composition in 1957. The two wanted to create an easily legible serif typeface for which the roman and italic styles were in perfect visual balance. Its name comes from the book in which it was first used: Giovanni Boccaccio's *Trattatello in Laude di Dante* ("Treatise in Praise of Dante," generally rendered into English as *Life of Dante*), published by the Officina Bodoni in 1955. In 1993, Monotype's Ron Carpenter redrew the type for digital use, and it continues to be a popular choice for books today.

HARPERVIA

An imprint dedicated to publishing international voices,
offering readers a chance to encounter other lives and other
points of view via the language of the imagination.

Turn this page for an excerpt from
Damilare Kuku's debut novel,
Only Big Bumbum Matters Tomorrow,
available from HarperVia beginning July 2024.

PROLOGUE

"I plan to renovate my bumbum in Lagos, live there for some time, and hopefully meet the love of my life!"

You had hoped your clever use of the word "renovate" would douse the tension in the room, elicit a smile from those assembled, perhaps even fits of laughter. Instead, you saw your mother digging her big toe into the old living room rug, the red nail paint chipping as she dug deeper.

Silence.

"Ehn? Témì, Sé o ti bèrè sí í mu igbó ni? Have you started smoking weed? Why would you do that?" Aunty Jummai barked at you while retying her wrapper. The smoke from the jollof rice cooking in the kitchen caused her eyes to water.

A ringtone was hastily silenced; someone muffled a cough. The lawyer who had been getting ready to take his leave sank deeper into the chair your father had loved.

"No, Aunty. Smoking kills. Would I fix my buttocks if I wanted to die young? I am doing it because I want to—it's my body," you answered as truthfully as you could.

Now you were stuck in the house, with no chance of fleeing the slow fire that was burning within your family. You were unlikely to make the consultation scheduled for ten days' time.

Nigerian families can be an obstacle in a girl's journey to a figure eight.

PART ONE

TODAY,
THIS SMALL YANSH
MUST GO!

TÉMÌ IS A BLACKBOARD

Your bumbum has always been flat.

You stared, as usual, hoping that some fat had miraculously found its way into it. In your midi midnight-blue lace dress, you looked at your slender frame in the full-length mirror that stood next to your bed. You lifted one hand to clutch both breasts and touched the small of your back with the other. If only your ass was bigger, your tiny waist would have been a magnet for compliments. You dropped both hands and sighed. This was your morning ritual. For yourself. For your sanity. For your sense of somebodiness.

You looked at the window opposite your bed and made a mental note to dust it and wash the curtains that hung loosely by its sides.

You thought about what you planned to do. You thought about your family.

You sighed again.

How do you inform your family members that you intend to surgically enlarge your buttocks without receiving a barrage of curses? How do you slip it into a conversation with Màámi that you intend to relocate to Lagos to meet the man who will love you senseless? How do you tell your older sister, who, until a week ago, you hadn't seen in five years, that you are hoping to stay in her Lagos apartment while you recover from surgery, maybe even stay a few more months? How?

These questions had been nagging at you since you decided to take the big step to redeem your backside. Time was not your friend; you needed to make the announcement quickly if you were to cash in on the new Easter discount you had seen on Instagram yesterday. The advertisement was clear and straight to the point:

Laydiz, this is for you!
This offer lasts till the end of the month.
So, if you really want to enter Easter with a snatched body,
Now is the time to go for it.
For my slim laydiz, BBL is possible!
For my thick laydiz, BBL is possible!
Fillers, BBL, nonsurgical butt lift . . . this clinic has got you!
Don't go to where they will not shape your yansh well o.

You loved the hearty salesmanship of the clinic's brand ambassador, even with her confusing accent and nude-glossed lips revealing the whitest teeth you had ever seen. She probably had veneers. You beamed at your phone using the screen as a mirror to assess your own teeth. They were not shockingly white, but white enough, thanks to your mother who brushed your teeth with pákò when you were a child, before using a toothbrush with toothpaste.

Good personal hygiene was a virtue that was nonnegotiable for Màámi. Her favourite quote had always been "A woman's parts should be clean and her breath fresh." She would scold you mildly whenever she noticed a speck of imperfection. "Témì, I can still see the soap on your body. Go back and give yourself another rinse. Ládùn, go and supervise your sister." Most times, the supervision ended in a splashing contest between you and your sister, until one of your parents broke it off. It was of utmost importance that you scrubbed thoroughly with kànrìnkàn and rinsed with water.

The bumbum-enlargement advert continued playing. The presenter, Sylvia Osuji, an alumna of your university, was now an influencer. She spoke glowingly of the ongoing Easter offer, sharing with great enthusiasm how she saved up for her surgery, how her decision to go under the knife was the best she had ever made, and how her ass now attracted the high-and-mighty. "Use what you have to get what you want," she crowed. Sylvia was an acquaintance in your university days, so you had no qualms about going to a clinic she had recommended. While Sylvia was a year ahead of you, she had never been high on the social ladder and mostly stayed in the shadows. However, since graduating, she had been winning in every circle, all because of that new ass.

The first time you saw her video, you sent it straight to your friend. "Bọ̀bọọ́lá, you know we are about to graduate. I think it's time we upgraded ourselves like Sylvia."

"Témì, I agree. I swear, I was just thinking about it. Dis my yansh no gree grow."

Her eagerness made you uneasy. "Don't you want to think about it?"

"Nope. I'm down," she responded.

"It's just our parents I'm worried about."

"Must they know? And as long as they are not paying, mine couldn't care less."

"Who will pay for yours?" you asked.

"You know that man that has been sending me messages on Twitter? I checked his profile. He has money. If he wants to date me, he will pay. Yours?"

"I am not sure."

"Témì, we have been confined to Ifè all our lives. If we must move, let us start making decisions on our own."

"Perhaps I could tell my daddy after we graduate. He's actually cool about these things. It is Màámi that could pose a challenge. For now, we should do proper research on the procedure. Maybe we should go with the clinic that Sylvia used."

"That clinic is expensive, Témì. Do you have three million naira? I don't think I can get more than one million from all my boyfriends combined. I hope this Twitter guy comes through. Let me start replying to his DMs now."

"Bọ̀bọọ́lá, please, let's just wait. We will find a way."

"Okay, we'll wait."

The verbal agreement clearly meant nothing to Bọ̀bọọ́lá because she resumed the final semester with an enlarged ass. "I ate a lot of protein during the Covid-19 break, and I wore a waist trainer every day," Bọ̀bọọ́lá told every girl who asked.

"Please share your diet with me. I need my backside to start confusing my boyfriend," your school friends pleaded.

You saw them perching around her like she was a messiah, hanging on her every word. You wondered if it was the protein that shaped her ass like a perfect apple and cinched her waist. Protein must have been a miracle worker that only favoured Bọ̀bọọ́lá. Bọ̀bọọ́lá's betrayal showed that you never really knew people, even if you had been best friends for over ten years.

This made her recent visits all the more unexpected. You didn't invite her or anyone else when your daddy died. At least *she* could claim that she used to be your friend; the others were mere neighbourhood acquaintances. One example was Solá, whose family had moved next door when his father became a professor, and to whom all you ever said was the occasional, half-hearted greeting.

The day you went with your parents to welcome them, Solá's mother said, "You people should be friends! Témì looks like a good girl. Just see how nice you look together." You knew this tired line well. The African parent's go-to attempt at subtle matchmaking.

You and Solá exchanged numbers, but you both knew it was unlikely either would get in touch. He was the sort of guy who moved with the club guys on campus, the ones whose parents sent them to federal universities to humble them but still gave them a comfortable-enough life to make up for not going abroad for university. Until recently, you had no reason to spend time together.

Thankfully, you were too busy with errands to deal with the unwelcome mourners. Besides, Ládùn's presence kept everyone's mouth busy. Hushed whispers travelled through the air every day whenever she showed her face at the house. The prodigal child had returned!

"Témì, is that Ládùn? Damn! She is so fine!" Solá had spoken into your left ear while everyone was singing the final hymn in church. The simp had forgotten that he was shoving his tongue down your throat just earlier that day. He had also forgotten funerals were not for flirting, or maybe he had never cared about decency.

"I am in love. Maybe *she* is the sister for me. *As you no gree for me.*"

"Solá, please sing the hymn," you hissed as the organ

struck a chord that had the choir singing louder, masking your reprimand. Your eyes travelled to Ládùn, who stood beside Màámi at the altar, where they were receiving prayers on behalf of the family.

Ládùn and Màámi could easily be mistaken for twins. They wore matching Ankara styles—body-fitting gowns with aso-oke adorning the fronts of their dresses. Although grief had given her a hunched back, Màámi's beauty was the kind you had to take in slowly and repeatedly, to be sure she was not a drawing. Graceful as a swan, Ládùn was not fair-skinned like your mother, but she also wasn't the colour of the night, as you were. She had your mother's face, but all her mannerisms were your father's. Trust Ládùn to steal the shine even after many years of being away. *Your* face was a perfect mix of your parents', and thankfully, you took each of their best features: your father's full lips and sleepy, catlike eyes and your mother's pointed nose and brownish-pink lips, but it didn't make people stare at you the way they stared at Màámi and Ládùn. If you didn't love your sister so much, you would have hated her.

Suddenly, your phone buzzed. Sylvia the Influencer had just posted another picture, showing her before-and-after bodies, reminding you of your present dilemma—how to inform your family of the decision to embellish your bumbum. You closed Instagram and opened the banking app to check your account balance. After saving for nearly two years, you had two million naira, thanks to a lucrative side hustle and Daddy's generosity.

At your graduation, a year before, your father had asked what you wanted, eager to reward you for your First-Class Honours, but you couldn't bring yourself to say it. Since Ládùn had left, they treated you like they were afraid you would leave too. Why else would anyone throw such a lavish graduation party and hire a famous musician like Yínká Ayéfẹlẹ, who only performed at big society events? The music from your party nearly drowned out other parents' celebrations. Ayéfẹlẹ serenaded the guests with the talking drum, singing your praises. Màámi sang along with him, giddy with excitement, like a schoolgirl.

> *Mo gbọ́ wípé many people*
> *Wón ní wí pé many people saaaayyyy . . .*
> *still Ayéfẹlẹ o le dìde*

"Màámi, must Yínká Ayéfẹlẹ sing so loudly?"

"Ehn ehn, would you rather he whispered? After we paid him so much?" She twirled under the rented canopy.

An hour into Ayéfẹlẹ's performance, other graduates came to the canopy that your family had installed in the middle of the field. They celebrated with you, resigned to the

fact that no one could outshine your mother. As you wel-
comed and served strangers, you remembered that Ládùn's
graduation was celebrated with a quiet dinner that your father missed because he was attending a ceremony with the
vice chancellor in Àkúré. Ládùn left for Lagos that night. Yet
here they were—giving out gift bags as souvenirs and smiling sheepishly.

"Témì, what do you want, dear?" your father repeated in
his airy voice. He was serious.

A new bumbum will be great, sir, you wanted to say. But you
replied, "I am fine, Daddy."

"Témì, come and dance with your mother," Màámi called.

"Màámi—" A lump formed in your throat as you hesi-
tated.

"Just come, my brilliant baby." Màámi dragged you to the
dance floor.

Aunty Jummai was serving food and receiving congratu-
latory messages as if she was the mother of the child graduating. Sometimes, you felt she acted outlandishly, hoping to
get a reaction from your mother. Your mother ignored her,
as usual.

You spent the rest of the day avoiding unsolicited prayers
from well-wishers. "After this graduation, your husband will
locate you!" "Children will locate you!" "You will find a good
job!" "You will get a visa to travel and leave this country!"
Their prayers were spoken in between mouthfuls of succulent

meat, while you tried your best to avoid their spittle hitting your forehead.

Amen!

The next time that you felt confident enough to tell your parents about your desired gift was a quiet evening after the usual family devotion. As your father relaxed into his chair, fanning himself with the newspaper he had read earlier in the day, Màámi and Aunty Jummai cracked melon seeds over a wooden tray at the dining table. You were seated close to your father in the living room.

"Daddy, Màámi, I want—"

Aunty Jummai cut in. "My professor, I have been meaning to discuss the recent strike with you—"

"Jummai, Témì was about to say something," Màámi interjected.

Aunty Jummai's eyes flared. "And I should keep quiet for her?"

Màámi got up as if scorched by Aunty Jummai's eyes and walked toward you.

"No, Màámi, it is not important." You were already tired.

"Are you sure?" Your daddy enquired with a smile. "Is it money?"

"No, I'll be in my room." Your exhaustion had peaked.

"Okay, dear. Let me give your dad and your aunty room to continue their conversation."

As you and your mother walked into the corridor, Aunty Jummai resumed. "They are also helping the government to waste their time. It is bad enough that the ASUU is always going on strike. Now the students want to join? A four-year course will soon be eight years with an extra year to deal with carryovers!"

"Hmmm. Sister Jummai, perhaps the students have the right to demand improved facilities and a better learning environment."

"Yes, they do, Prof, but they won't get those things! This is Nigeria. They should stop dreaming."

You could hear the conversation from your room, so you turned to TikTok videos of post-surgery recovery tips until your eyes gave way to sleep. So you didn't tell them that night either.

Then your father died.

Your father's burial ceremony was scheduled to be a three-day event. On the first day, strange, noisy relatives arrived in hordes and filled your three-bedroom bungalow on Road Seven at the university staff quarters. All dressed in black, the association of wailing aunties was the loudest, occasionally hitting high notes.

"Titó ooooo. Titó has left us. Our only brother!" As the day dissolved into evening, they put their bags in the corner of the living room.

"Témì, please take us where we will sleep. It is good we are staying here. I need to feed you. You are so slim—you need to chop up."

"Ma?"

Màámi waded in. "I am sure she is excited to eat your food, Ma, so she can put on weight. Témì, go and drop their bags in your room." Her eyes pleaded with you to keep quiet.

Later that evening, as you folded your clothes in Màámi's bedroom, you challenged her. "Màámi, why can't these people stay in hotels? Why are we all packed in here like sardines?"

"Témì, your mouth is too sharp. They are family."

"Family members whose names you don't know?"

"Please, go and help Aunty Jummai in the kitchen and let me be."

Your home felt like a face-me-I-face-you apartment with really loud neighbours. The two toilets were always in use. You ended up going over to Solá's house to relieve yourself. He seemed to take your using his restroom as an invitation to bombard you with solicitous text messages.

Hey Témì, I am really sorry about your dad.

Please feel free to come to my house to chill.

We can stay in my room, doing nothing.

. . .

By the way, this is Solá, your neighbour,

in case you didn't save my number.

You took him up on his invite, and his room became your hideout. After two days of lying side by side in awkward silence, hopping from one social media platform to another, you asked him to show you how to French kiss. Who knew kissing involved so much saliva? "Solá, whatever you do, don't touch my breasts!"

"I know all this is trauma bonding, but if you ever feel like taking this further—" he whispered against your lips.

"Solá, please shut up," you cut in. "You know I don't mess with quarters boys. Who is taking what further with you? Please, let us focus. Kiss me. I want to try biting."

The second day of the burial ceremony was the hardest. You stood between your sister and your mother when they lowered your father into the ground. You saw tears trickle down Ládùn's cheeks onto her búbù, and your mother just kept muttering your father's name. Didn't they know your father was always going to be around? Just not in physical form.

Later that day, you were in charge of topping up the firewood for the caterers and the aunties who had joined them. You listened to the family gossip they shared with one another, forgetting that you were seated in a corner, avoiding the smoke from the stove. You discovered many things that day.

Apparently, your mother was not the woman your father was supposed to marry, but the moment he met your mother, he forgot about the other woman.

"The woman he jilted refused to marry anyone else. She had hoped that Titó would eventually come back to her. It is her, Ęlẹ́da, that is avenging herself by killing him. I heard he didn't even go anywhere—Covid just walked in and sat in his body gbam."

"That poor woman," another aunt chimed in. "I send her wishes and prayers at the start of every month because I was the one that introduced them. I feel responsible for her spinsterhood." She blew on the piece of ram she had taken from the caterer's bowl.

"My dear sister, that other woman can't compare to Hassana. Hassana is beautiful. That other woman's teeth alone! Have you seen the arrangement? That woman needs a dentist, not a professor."

"Let us leave that matter. Please, have you seen Lara?"

Your ears stood at attention at the mention of Big Mummy. You were more than interested in hearing your aunt's backstory, and the tidbits were coming hard and fast.

"Her skin looks like it is going through a midlife crisis."

"My dear, the bleaching that woman does is abnormal!"

"Have you seen that small boy she calls her husband?"

"When Titó married that Hausa woman, he abandoned his family."

"Goodness knows what they gave him to eat. It's as if he forgot he was someone's big brother."

"With nobody to control Lara, she has just been going from man to man."

You did not get much sleep that night because you were sharing your room with Ìyá Ámúsà, who was the last of the guests to leave. Just when you thought she couldn't snore any louder, she increased the volume. You sighed and went over to Solá's place, where he offered you some edibles.

"I know you like to appear tough, Témì, but your dad's death hit every one of us. So just let it out. Udoka's cookies are legendary." Solá bit into one of the cookies and held out another.

"How that guy runs a whole weed business from his parents' boys' quarters without their knowledge amazes me," you said.

"He is cashing out big-time! He sells online. I buy from him on Snapchat. You just send him a private message, and he sends one of his delivery guys," Sola said.

"You know I don't like that stuff. Besides, we have a big day tomorrow. My father's lawyer is coming to read the will."

"This will help, I promise."

You ate the cookies because they were delicious. After

that, you began another kissing session. He sucked your tongue like he was hungry, and you nibbled gently on his lips, taking intermittent breaks to catch your breath. Soon, you both lost track of time.

It was Aunty Jummai's voice that woke you at daybreak. "Témì! Food is ready! Come and eat!"

"I have to go," you said, wiping the sleep from your eyes.

"Do you want to go out for ice cream later?"

"No, Solá. My father just died. Ice cream is the last thing on my mind." You saw his face fall, so you quickly added, "Thank you, though. See you tomorrow."

"Sure thing. Sorry." His voice sounded hollow, and his head grew bigger.

You stopped in the doorway to lean on the frame. "Solá, this thing you gave me, is it strong?"

"Nah. You only had three cookies. You will be fine."

As you walked home, your house receded farther into the distance. You picked up your pace until you reached the kitchen door.

"You didn't hear me calling you?" Aunty Jummai demanded as she stood in the kitchen, holding your plate out to you. Was that custard and moin-moin or oats with àkàrà? Everything looked blurry.

"Take it from my hand now. If you are going to be playing cat and mouse with your food as usual, please just leave it. There are too many mouths to feed," she said pointedly.

"Thank you, Ma."

"I know you won't listen. Why do I even bother? Coconut head." She shook her head.

"Thank you, Aunty."

You stopped at the dining area to do exactly what she had warned you not to do. By the time you disappeared into the privacy of your bedroom, different versions of you emerged from the shadows. You felt like you were in that *Matrix* movie your father loved.

"Keanu Reeves is a gem, I tell you. He is like our Richard Mofe-Damijo—both of them gems! Those guys," he would say during family movie night.

"My love, please be quiet. I still don't understand this film." Your mother would shush him so you could all watch the movie for the hundredth time, the entire family cozied up on the sofa.

Focus, Témì! When are you telling them? A version of you who was sitting at the end of the bed interrupted your thoughts.

"I am going to tell them tomorrow!" you replied.

Why would you tell them at all? Màámi will lose it, said another you who was leaning against the door.

Tell them! Tell them! The other three versions of you, who were scattered across the room, egged you on.

"Témì! Please come out, the lawyer is here." Màámi's voice interrupted your conversation.

You headed to the living room, hearing voices. A spicy aroma from the kitchen teased your nose. As you floated down the corridor, you felt happier than you had been in the last fourteen days since your father died. Your mother must have arranged for the reading to happen immediately after the internment. She knew Ládùn could take off at any time.

You sat and watched as Big Mummy, Màámi, Ládùn, and Aunty Jummai listened to the lawyer read your father's will. It felt like everyone else was floating too.

The living room was filled with faces that were worn from tears and despair, the same living room where your father had danced with you so many times.

"I will show you that I can still boogie," he always boasted.

"Daddy, nobody says 'boogie' anymore."

"Ahh, sorry. I will show you I am a stepper," he would respond as he zigzagged through the air, throwing his arms everywhere, a move that never failed to make Màámi and Ládùn burst into fits of laughter.

Barrister Chima started on a solemn note. "Good afternoon. Once again, I am sorry for your loss. No matter what is read today, please know that Titó loved you all so much. He asked me to say this."

"Lawyer, we know he loved us. Please, let us move fast; you know I am staying in town." Big Mummy pointed her talons toward the door, as if town was a place too far away to describe.

"Please, let him speak," Aunty Jummai said.

The two women looked at each other, each picking the other person up with her eyes and slamming her onto the ground.

The lawyer cleared his throat loudly, his Adam's apple bobbing up and down. You wanted to walk over and touch it to make it stop. His forehead suddenly looked too large. Perhaps he should have considered surgery himself. Forehead surgery.

He began to list everything your father had acquired in his lifetime. He left his house in Ìgboyà, five million naira, the car, and some of his clothes to your mother. He left two million naira, his farm, and some of his books to your sister. He left you the rest of his books, and the guinea brocade shirts you always borrowed, and one million naira. To Aunty Jummai, he left five hundred thousand naira. As the lawyer kept reading, your mother stole glances at Ládùn, and Aunty Jummai sniggered at Big Mummy, as if to say, *After everything, he left you nothing!*

"And that is it. As you know, Prof wasn't the richest man. He was a public servant. However, he made some investments in agritech, and we are hopeful that they will yield returns, which he also willed to your mother." The lawyer put the document back into the folder. His left hand shook, showing his nervousness.

"Wow, wow, wow, Màámi, your husband loved you o."

You had meant this to be a private thought, but from the wary eyes that immediately looked back at you, you realised you had spoken out loud.

"Thank you all for honouring your father's memory," Màámi stated at a high pitch, as if she had just sucked air from a helium balloon.

Barrister Chima, who everyone knew was waiting for the jollof rice, busied himself with shuffling his files as though he was about to leave.

"Lawyer, don't go yet, please. Let me pack something for you to take away," Aunty Jummai said.

"Your father would have been happy to see us together as a family. So, girls, what are your plans?" Màámi continued.

Silence.

"I am not sure," Ládùn said quietly.

"I assume you are not staying to monitor the farm your father left you."

"Mum, I am sure you are more than capable of sorting that out."

"Farming was you and your father's way of bonding. I know nothing about it."

"He is dead, and I can't do it alone. There are people who actually want this, so please give it to them."

You looked at Ládùn. Her hands were clutching her bag as if she was waiting on an alarm so she could escape.

"What about the house in Ìgboyà?" Màámi asked softly, afraid that Ládùn's next answer might cut even deeper. "I can't look after it by myself."

"Mum, please, you can manage the tenants. If the house needs renovating, we can always discuss that. Let's talk about this later. I am still around for a while."

"Oh, I thought you were leaving after this. No problem, then." Your mother and your sister both looked in different directions.

Big Mummy was staring at her talons, evidently not pleased that her brother had left her out of his will. Aunty Jummai was tapping her feet, probably thanking God for the money your father had left her. The lawyer had started packing his papers into the bag but was being deliberately slow. Everyone's minds had wandered away from the meeting. You figured you might as well just tell them now that they were sombre, so your mother could deal with the pain in one go. You decided the meeting was the perfect opportunity to kill two birds with one stone.

It was either this or send it in the family WhatsApp group, which had been created two weeks earlier and had already become Aunty Jummai's favourite place to send Bible verses, long broadcast audio/video messages, and badly angled, blurry pictures.

You decided to just say it.

Ládùn didn't look at you, but you saw the way her narrow nose twitched and her nostrils flared, which convinced you she had heard. *Good. Now we can all see that everyone in this family can be mad.*

"I don't understand. Is there an injury on your bumbum?" Màámi asked with genuine concern. "Why didn't you tell me, my dear?"

Ládùn's shoulders shook slightly.

"No, Màámi, I am going to get myself a bumbum, like that woman on TV that you always talk about."

"All the women on TV now have big bumbum, Témì. Be straight, please."

"I am going to get a Brazilian butt lift."

"A what? You are going to Brazil?"

"I am adding fat to my buttocks, Màámi."

"I still don't understand! What is wrong with your bumbum exactly?" Màámi asked, looking puzzled.

"It is flat!" you said.

"Was it big before?"

"No, that's why I am going to enlarge it."

Màámi started laughing, but the lines of grief on her face became more pronounced. "Témì, please, this is not the right time to crack jokes. What does your bumbum have to do with your father's death?"

"Màámi, you are the one who asked about our plans—"

Your mother raised her hand. "Témì, please, if you are having a hard time coping with your father's death, I can understand that. You can take a holiday to Lagos. But you are not moving to Lagos, nor are you doing whatever to your buttocks."

"It is not really your decision to make, Màámi. I am an adult."

There was a sinister look on Màámi's face that you had never seen before. She looked up to the ceiling as if to summon your dead father to restrain her from dashing across the room to strangle you.

"You don't know what you are talking about, Témì." Ládùn finally spoke.

"Were you not twenty when you decided to leave the house and never return? *I* am almost twenty-one!"

"We are not talking about your sister, please!" Aunty Jummai cut in.

"Why shouldn't we? She's sitting here, acting like she hasn't been away for five years." Ládùn's eyes met yours. Your recent car conversations came to mind, and you felt yourself thaw.

"Témì, your father has not even been in the ground for a day, and you are already showing your true colours," Aunty Jummai said.

Màámi turned to face you. "Témì, do you want to kill me? You want me to join your father so soon?"

Big Mummy seemed pleased that karma was already biting her brother in the ass. "Let me be on my way. This seems like a private family matter." She moved her frame to the edge of the seat.

"Ahn ahn! Big Mummy, you are their mother as well. You are part of this conversation." Màámi clutched her sister-in-law's arm and turned back to Témì. "Young lady, who do you even know in Lagos? Where will you stay?"

"I was working my way up to it, Màámi." You turned to your sister. "Ládùn, this is why I wanted to come to your place. Please, can I stay with you in Lagos?"

"Témì, shut your small mouth," Big Mummy interjected.

Aunty Jummai suddenly found her voice again. "Is this what that friend of yours did? That one that came to the burial with the big yansh that did not rhyme with her body. Is it because we didn't disgrace her?"

"Jummai, please wait, is that what her friend did?" Màámi wanted to know, still struggling to make sense of your announcement.

"It must be! Did you not see how her yansh shot out like a misfired bullet?"

"Ah! I thought she had put on weight. Témì, is that what you want to look like?" Màámi asked quietly.

"Jesus! Why our family?" Aunty Jummai clapped her hands and screamed.

Barrister Chima chipped in. "Témì, it is possible that there are legal restrictions on a girl your age going under the knife. I must investigate this." The long-awaited jollof rice was no longer a sufficient reason to remain in the middle of the family commotion.

"Témì wants me to join her father! She wants to kill me!" Your mother leaned on the right arm of your father's favourite chair.

Big Mummy yanked off her head tie and flung it across the room, then ran to pick it up immediately. She circled the sofa, screaming, "La ilaha illallah! They have got Témì! They have got her!"

"Let's look at all the women seated here," you started.

They all looked at one another; only Ládùn looked straight ahead.

You continued. "I can't help but wonder whether it is people from your family that cast a spell on me, Màámi. Why did they not do the same to Ládùn? You all have big butts. I am the only one in the family with a tiny behind. I am going to fix it. I was going to ask you for money to add to my savings because I need compression garments—they call them fája—but I guess from your reaction that none of you will be willing to assist."

They looked increasingly shocked as you spoke; the silence was palpable. The ceiling fan was suddenly louder than the voices in your head. "Aunty Jummai, the rice you are cooking is burning," you blurted out.

As if on cue, Aunty Jummai started crying while Big Mummy gathered her things and hurried toward the door. Màámi sat staring at you while Ládùn looked as though she wanted to be a fly on the wall in a different house. She really had become a stranger.

The harmattan in Ilé-Ifẹ̀ was still raging that night, although it was late February. As you drowsily searched for the blanket you had kicked off while you slept, you caught a glimpse of your mother, who was sitting at the edge of the bed. Why did Màámi look like she had two heads and four necks? That Udoka deserved a special place in hell.

Màámi had a habit of bending over you at night, either in prayer or tending to you when you were sick. She had started doing it after Ládùn left. She wasn't a religious person, but she began praying for her children and husband. Then, when your father fell sick, she switched to fervent midnight prayers.

"God can hear me better when most people are sleeping. Besides, Jummai's prayers begin at three a.m., and I have to finish before she begins the war with her enemies."

"Màámi!" Your raspy voice made her jerk upright. She looked at you and sighed. There were heavy bags under her eyes.

"Témì, what is wrong with your bumbum? You can tell me. I am a woman like you. I can help."

"Hmmm . . ." You rubbed your eyes, hoping to chase sleep away, then rested your head on your other hand.

"Why would you say you are moving to Lagos and fixing your bumbum?"

"I am not leaving permanently. I just want to see Lagos. Màámi, you came here because you fell in love with Daddy. What if my destiny is in Lagos?"

"With a new bumbum?" Her voice shook a little. "You realise this won't draw men to you? Is that what this is about?"

"No. I am doing it for me."

"Isn't that what killed Stella Obásanjó? She went under the knife and died. So you want me to lose my husband and then lose my child?"

"Màámi, medical science has evolved. I have done the research. The doctor comes highly recommended, and the patients he has operated on have been just fine."

"Where will you get the money?"

"I have savings."

"How much?"

"Errr . . ." You stuttered.

"Témì, how much?"

"Almost two million naira."

"Ahhh! Did you steal it?"

"No, Màámi, I have been saving for a while—and you know I sell hair extensions. Aunty Jummai helped me to start that business at the beginning of the pandemic."

"My dear, I was there when Jummai gave you that money. So you started a hair business so that you can have funds to fix your buttocks. What a wonder!"

"Màámi, please try to understand. I would appreciate it if you could assist me with some extra money to help me survive in Lagos."

"So I should give you money to go and kill yourself?"

"I need money for post-recovery care. I will have to buy some undergarments."

"Témì, I don't understand this. What am I missing? Are you angry with me?"

"Màámi, this is not about you. I would have added breast enlargement to my quest, but thankfully, I have boobs."

"My dear daughter, it is very much about me. I am your mother; every decision you take affects me."

You wondered if you should ask her why she didn't talk Ládùn out of leaving, but you decided not to. "No. It is about me alone."

"You are not coping well with your father's death. There is no other explanation for this," she said. "What about NYSC? Are you not planning to serve your country as expected? You know no one will employ you if you don't finish that first. Is it during your service year that you will be fixing your bumbum? Ehn? While you are teaching or working in a village?" As she continued, the second head on her shoulder started to look like your father. *Who asked you to eat those cookies?*

"Màámi, I will be done with my surgery soon. You know all the nonacademic staff are on strike again. The government will waste their time for a few months, pretending they will cave, then the staff will go back to work. I have enough time to do it and recover. I will probably be called up with the Batch C."

"Témì the Wise. You have it all figured out. Go to sleep."

"Good night, Màámi."

"Good night."

As she closed the door, you thought of how you would cope with the reality of your father's demise. You had dealt with Ládùn's mysterious disappearance five years before, and you would deal with your father's death as well, after fixing your bumbum.